P9-DEU-727

7/02

LP
F
Hoag

Hoag, Tami

Heart of Dixie

DATE	ISSUED TO
MAR 2 7 2009	

SEP 1 2 2008

Heart of Dixie

Also by Tami Hoag
in Large Print:

Cry Wolf
Dust to Dust
Guilty as Sin
Lucky's Lady
Mismatch
Night Sins

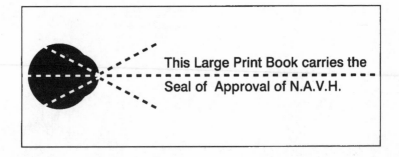

This Large Print Book carries the
Seal of Approval of N.A.V.H.

Heart of Dixie

Tami Hoag

Thorndike Press • Waterville, Maine

Published in 2002 by arrangement with Bantam Books, an imprint of The Bantam Dell Publishing Group, a division of Random House, Inc.

Thorndike Press Large Print Famous Authors Series.

The tree indicium is a trademark of Thorndike Press.

The text of this Large Print edition is unabridged.
Other aspects of the book may vary from the original edition.

Set in 16 pt. Plantin by Christina S. Huff.

Printed in the United States on permanent paper.

Library of Congress Cataloging-in-Publication Data

Hoag, Tami.
    Heart of Dixie / Tami Hoag.
        p.   cm.
    ISBN 0-7862-3487-3 (lg. print : hc : alk. paper)
    1. Southern States — Fiction.   2. Journalists — Fiction.
    3. Large type books.   I. Title.
    PS3558.O333 H43 2002
    813'.54—dc21   2001034757

With thanks to Betina Krahn, Pamela Bauer, and Candace Schuler, who were there for me the day my Firebird died on the way to Elk River.

And with fond thoughts of Leo's Magnolia Bar and Bob Dog, wherever you are.

One

The Porsche sped along the coastal highway north of Charleston. Jake Gannon sat back in the butter-soft leather seat, his right hand on the steering wheel, his left arm resting on the frame of the open window. To his right, the Atlantic stretched into infinity, bluer than the sky and dotted with whitecaps. The cool air that blew through the car was scented with the crisp tang of the sea.

On one level Jake could appreciate the beauty around him. But for the most part his mind was focused on more important things. Jake Gannon tackled every task with an eye to perfection. So far, perfection concerning this business wasn't even a dot on the horizon. The trail had gone utterly cold. It was as if Devon Stafford had simply ceased to exist.

The need for discretion was making his task difficult as he homed in on the area she might have run to. He couldn't flat out ask anyone if they had seen her because questions that blatant would alert too many people, not the least of whom might be Ms. Stafford herself. But he would gladly suffer the inconvenience of anonymity if it meant being the one to find the missing actress and chronicle the story of her rise to fame and her subsequent flight from it.

In three short years Devon Stafford had rocketed to the top, from would-be star to household name. She had become America's darling of both the large and small screen, scoring three big wins in feature films and landing her own weekly television series — *Wylde Time*, the tales of Chyna Wylde, trauma surgeon and amateur sleuth. She had become the latest idol to emulate, the world's newest icon of sex appeal and glamor. And then she had vanished.

All that was known was that she had argued with her producers over having gained a couple of pounds when she'd quit smoking. Hardly a reason to turn her back on success, but she had gone nevertheless. No one had seen or heard from her in a year.

As a biographer, Jake had to unearth the secrets of people like Devon Stafford. Not to expose them in the way of the tabloid reporters, but to find out what made them tick, to bring to the surface all the hidden dreams, the emotions that drove them, the pasts that haunted them; to show both their polished surfaces and the hairline cracks that ran beneath those surfaces. To present the famous to their public as ordinary people who had for whatever reason become larger-than-life legends.

It was a career he more or less had fallen into, but he had discovered in short order that he was good at it and that he liked it. For the past six years, ever since leaving the Marine Corps, he had made his living at it, writing as A. J. Campion. He saved his own name for the day when he would finally get a mystery novel sold and published. Mystery was his first love, but biographies were in some cases mysteries in their own right. Like now. Devon Stafford was a mystery, one he had every intention of solving.

Never mind that people had hunted for her like bloodhounds the first few months after her disappearance from Hollywood. *He* was going to find her. Devon Stafford was his objective, and with the thorough perfectionism he was known for, he had dug for every scrap, every tidbit of information about her, no matter how insignificant, no matter how trivial. When Jake Gannon set an objective, he attained it. Period.

He admitted having personal reasons for wanting to be the one to find the actress and convince her to tell her story through him.

He had been captivated by Devon Stafford the first time he'd seen her on a movie screen. She was drop-dead gorgeous with her wild waist-long mane of thick icy blond waves, her vibrant green eyes and bee-stung lips that begged a man to kiss them. Her body was the stuff of dreams — reed-slender and strong with subtle curves. She was Venus in a leotard. She was Aphrodite. She was perfect. Like every other red-blooded man on the planet, he felt his hormones go on overload every time he watched her on the screen.

But there was something else about her that made her special. Beautiful women weren't difficult to find. There were plenty of beautiful women who never achieved the kind of fame Devon Stafford had. There was something else about her, an intangible, a special something that made her seem almost incandescent on the screen. She had a way of touching the heart of every person watching her. It was that special something Jake most wanted to try to capture in print. He wanted to examine the puzzle that was Devon Stafford and explain her to the world in a way that would make all the pieces fall into place.

But first he had to find her.

Suddenly the Porsche gave a lurch and

sent up a racket that sounded as if someone were hammering under the hood. Jake bolted forward on his seat, muscles in his broad shoulders tensing to the hardness of granite, his eyes intently searching the gauges for signs of distress. The temperature gauge had gone off the scale. The sports car gave another buck and a cough and steam began to billow out from under the hood.

"Don't you dare," Jake commanded in a low, tight voice.

His big hands tightened on the steering wheel in a punishing grip. He glanced around quickly to see where he was. Somewhere between Nowhere and Oblivion; nothing but ocean and empty road as far as the eye could see. Damn, damn, and triple damn. Ahead a green sign indicated the exit to a place called Mare's Nest and he breathed a small sigh of relief.

"If you get me to Mare's Nest I'll buy you a new bug guard," he promised. "I'll rub leather conditioner into all your upholstery. I'll hand-polish every wheel spoke."

The Porsche rolled off the highway and down a two-lane road. Ahead lay rippling dunes set with stringy grass. Three or four miles ahead, sitting out on the tip of a little thumb of land jutting into the Atlantic, was

Mare's Nest. So close and yet so far.

"Come on, come on," Jake chanted, moving in his seat like an oversize jockey trying to urge a little more out of his mount. The Porsche would not be coaxed. It shuddered and hissed and locked up its power steering as its engine shut down altogether. The car lunged off the road and sank its front wheels rim-deep into the soft white sand.

Jake hurled himself out of the vehicle and stood beside it, glaring at it, as if he could intimidate it into starting again just with the ferocity of his scowl. It didn't work. The car hissed at him like a cat. Growling, he gave in to the urge to kick a tire. Then he calmed himself with an iron will and did the only thing he could do in view of the fact that he had absolutely no skill with machines. He climbed back inside the car, reached for his cellular phone, and prayed that Mare's Nest had a tow truck.

Dixie hummed along with a Bonnie Raitt tape, feeling supremely free and happy. It was Friday. The pale winter sun was fast sinking in the west. The day had been pleasantly warm, but cooler weather was rolling in. It was going to be a perfect night to bundle up and take a walk along the deserted beach, then snuggle up on the couch with a quilt, a book, and a big mug of rich hot chocolate. Maybe Sylvie Lieberman would come up to the house for a game of Scrabble. Maybe Dixie would be able to coax her cousin down from the attic for dinner. Regardless, it was going to be a fine evening. All was right with her world.

She shifted down for the curve and the big truck growled and rumbled up the gradual incline, purring as if it recognized the victim it had come to rescue. Dixie whistled under her breath at the sight of the sleek midnight blue Porsche 928S$_4$. Very nice. Not the car to suit her needs at the moment, but very nice indeed. It was also very motionless.

Flipping on the truck's flashing yellow beacon, she passed the Porsche and pulled over behind the stranded car. California plates, she noted with a slight frown. Probably a tourist.

She climbed down and rounded the hood, getting her first look at the car's owner. He had emerged from the shell of sleek metal and tinted glass and had stopped in mid-stride to stare at her. His handsome mouth hung open. He looked to be the quintessential California male: mid-thirties, perfectly good-looking in a perfectly blond, All-American way, with a perfect body decked out in perfect clothes. Big, broad-shouldered, slim-hipped, he looked like ninety percent of the men she'd known in California, only cuter. There was something irresistible and sweet in the look of utter confusion that knitted his brows together above his aviator sunglasses. The sea breeze fluttered through his straight golden hair, tossing it carelessly over his forehead. He glanced briefly at his car, giving Dixie a view of a strong profile that was rugged and tanned. Robert Redford had nothing on this guy.

"Oh, no, Dixie," she whispered under her breath as a dangerous feeling of weakness ribboned through her. "No California men for you."

As if he would even be interested, she thought with a mix of satisfaction and disappointment. Men who looked like that liked women of the Barbie doll variety, which she was not and had no desire to be.

"What happened here, sugar?" she drawled, strolling past him. She stopped at the nose of the Porsche and planted her hands on her hips, her gaze going from man to car as if an answer from either would satisfy her. "You blow a hose? A belt? Or is it something worse?"

He stared at her suspiciously for a long

moment before finding his voice. "I called for a tow truck," he said stupidly.

Dixie smiled. "And you got one. It's that big red and white thing with the flashing light on top and the cables and winches and boom all stickin' up out the back."

His gaze flicked over his shoulder to the truck and back again. Once more, those straight golden brows pulled together in consternation. His square chin jutted forward aggressively. He jammed his hands at the waist of his tailored tan slacks. "But you're a woman."

"So I've been told."

"I'm not a chauvinist," he declared, his frown darkening, challenging her to refute his statement. "I swear I'm not. I just wasn't expecting you to be a woman, that's all. I firmly believe women should have equality in the workplace."

"Just as long as they don't monkey around with your Porsche?" Dixie suggested sweetly.

A growl rumbled in Jake's chest. Lord, it was enough of a blow to his ego that he had to call for help. It galled him no end that he wasn't mechanical. That it was a woman coming to his rescue was rubbing salt into an old irrational wound. Now he had to choke down the unpleasant fact that he was a sexual bigot as well.

He looked the woman up and down, trying to see if her appearance was a clever disguise. She was around thirty, of medium height with an hourglass figure housed in snug jeans and a soft-looking brown sweater that emphasized the shape and size of her breasts. Her face was oval with a straight little nose and a pert little bow of a mouth. Wild and wavy nut brown hair had been sheered off at the bottom of her earlobes in a thick bob.

She wasn't at all the kind of woman he usually went for or even looked at twice, but as she gazed up at him with a wry twinkle in her hazel eyes, he felt the unmistakable stirring of desire. A lazy, warm stirring deep in his gut. Strange. It probably had to do with the trauma of his situation. He admitted she was cute in a well-fed sort of way, but he tried to shove aside the attraction even as it took a firmer hold on him. She was cute, but that didn't qualify her to touch his Porsche.

He didn't have children because he had yet to find the perfect wife. He didn't have a dog because he traveled too much. But he had his Porsche and all his considerable possessive, protective instincts had directed themselves at the car. He wasn't keen on letting just anybody touch it.

"What happened to Eldon of Eldon's Gas

and Go?" he asked at length. He shoved his sunglasses on top of his head and fixed the woman with a gaze that had persuaded more than one Marine to confess to some minor misdeed.

Dixie's breath evaporated in her lungs. His eyes were as blue as the ocean on a cloudless day, intense, electric blue, perfectly blue. Naturally. She glanced away from him to compose herself, righting her sense of calm control with an effort that wasn't altogether successful. Luckily, she was good at covering for herself.

"He's gone up to Dongola for Buzz and Fayrene Taylor's forty-fifth wedding anniversary party. Won't be back till Monday. Fayrene is Eldon's wife's sister," she explained, her heartbeat picking up at the look in the man's eyes. A girl could drown in all that blue. He really was awfully handsome. She'd always had a weakness for a big strapping man. Even his scowl struck her as cute.

"His gout is acting up something fierce anyway," she added absently, her gaze riveted to Jake's mouth. "Like as not if he was here he'd of sent me, 'cause Junior is gone to watch the Whippets play basketball."

She took a step back from him and drew in a deep breath of cool air in another attempt to clear her head. Swinging a hand in the direction of the Porsche, she said, "Can we pop the hood on this little sweetheart? It's gonna be gettin' dark."

Jake stepped in front of the car, insinuating himself between the woman and his beloved Porsche, trying to shield it as a father would his child. "Let's not be hasty," he said with a tight smile. "Maybe she just needs a little rest."

Dixie gave him a look. "Honey, it's a car, not a Thoroughbred."

"That's your opinion."

She rolled her eyes and propped her hands on her hips. "You may not believe this, but next to Eldon I'm probably the most mechanical person in Mare's Nest. Now try to look past the fact that I'm wearing a bra and tell me what the car was doing before it quit."

Jake thought it was nearly impossible to overlook the fact that she wore a bra. He doubted anyone else at Eldon's Gas and Go filled their shirt out quite the way she did. His heart gave a jolt as his gaze settled on her ample bosom. He decided to explain his car problems if for no reason other than to distract himself from imagining just what kind of bra it was she had on under that sweater.

"Well . . . there was this hammering noise and then it did this kind of chukka-chukka thing and a big white cloud came out from under the hood."

This news was met with a pained expression. "How far did you drive it after that?"

"Not far. A couple of miles." She grimaced and he recanted. "No, wait, maybe it was only a mile or a few hundred yards. It probably just seemed farther. And I was coasting most of the way. I'm sure it just got a little hot. It's probably fine."

"You're not real handy with cars, are you." It was more a statement than a question.

Jake's male pride bristled. He squared his wide shoulders and set his jaw at a truculent angle, but the only argument he could come back with was a juvenile-sounding, "So?"

His inability with machines had been apparent from an early age. He had landed himself in the emergency room the very day he'd been given his first — and last — Erector Set. People who knew him generally avoided being anywhere in the vicinity when he was working with anything that remotely resembled a power tool.

He considered his lack of mechanical talent a terrible flaw in his character, one he had cursed and puzzled over his whole life. He might have declared up and down that he wasn't a chauvinist, but the fact of the matter was, he had the idea engraved on his brain that men were supposed to be good with machines and he was not. He was a man's man, an athlete's athlete, and he was having to surrender his Porsche to a curvy brunette. It rankled big time and all he could do was scowl.

Shaking her head, his lady rescuer shooed him aside, not intimidated in the least. She released the catch and lifted the hood on the Porsche. Jake watched her poke around at the engine, checking belts and hoses, making the kind of significant humming sounds doctors make when they really want to worry a person sick.

"Are you *sure* you know what you're doing?" he asked, his hands itching to pull her away from his baby.

"Hmmm . . . ummm . . ." She bent over into the guts of the car, sticking her heart-shaped fanny up as she tried to scoot down closer to a malevolent-looking appendage with wires sticking out of it.

Jake's attention momentarily drifted from the car to the derriere. Her sweater had ridden up around her waist, revealing age-thinned denim that hugged a delightfully rounded rear. He was traditionally a leg man, but this angle was giving him a whole new perspective on the female form. He would have enjoyed the view a whole lot more if the woman hadn't been clanging a wrench around inside his pride and joy, however. He winced and groaned as if she were twisting his own body parts. Then she straightened, dug a small oily rag out of her front pocket and carefully opened the car's radiator cap.

"Hmmm . . ."

His heartbeat quickened. He pushed the image of her fanny from his mind and leaned beside her over the engine. "What? That sounded more ominous than the other 'hmms.' What is it?"

"Hmmm . . ."

Dixie turned her head. He was right there. Close enough for her to catch the scent of mint on his breath. Close enough to see three different shades of gold in his hair and the faint shadow of his beard on the hard planes of his cheeks. Close enough to lean over and kiss if she were to completely lose all common sense.

"There's nothing in your radiator," she whispered breathlessly, desire grabbing her by the throat.

He blinked at her, looking a little mesmerized, then he shook his head and cleared his throat. "That's bad," he mumbled, his gaze straying to her lips. "Even I know that's bad. What do we do?"

Trying to shake off the spell of his closeness, Dixie replaced the radiator cap, motioned him back and closed the hood. "Nothing to do but haul her in and have a better look. Could be the water pump, could be a hose down underneath, could be a puncture in the radiator." She looked up at him with a grave, earnest expression. "You might have blown the engine."

A pitiful sound of dread and suffering caught in his throat. He paled visibly beneath his tan. Dixie patted his arm consolingly. Poor thing. Poor cute thing. She wanted to give him a hug, but thought better of it. Instead, she went to the tow truck to prepare to load the car.

Jake wobbled on his feet at the thought of a blown engine. Lord, what would Andre say when he got back to L.A.? The mechanic treated all of his client's cars as if they were children. He was an import auto pediatrician, recommended from car owner to car owner by reverent word of mouth. He had purred over Jake's new Porsche. A blown engine. It would probably reduce the Frenchman to tears. Jake shuddered at the thought.

The sound of hydraulic wheezing broke in on his thoughts and he bolted toward the back of his car. Long iron spear-like things were emerging from the tow truck, the kind of things he'd seen run through junkers in order to lift them onto the scrap heap. His imagination raced ahead to picture the rods impaling his Porsche. Control snapping, he flung himself spread-eagle on the car. "No! Please! Anything but that!"

Dixie shook her head and sighed, working the levers, lowering the bars that would slide under the car's rear wheels and lift the vehicle off the ground. "You'll have to move, now, honey, else you'll be squashed. You're welcome to sit up in the cab of the truck if it's too painful for you to watch."

Embarrassed beyond words, Jake stormed up to the wrecker and climbed in on the passenger's side. What was the matter with him? Where was his pride? He'd managed to make a perfect ass of himself. The woman obviously knew what she was doing. He of all people knew mechanical ability had nothing to do with gender. It was just that she looked so . . . soft. He wouldn't have expected a female wrecker driver to be quite so . . . female.

"Jeez, Gannon, what would you expect? Arnold Schwarzenegger with breasts?" he growled, shaking his head in self-reproach, and turned his thoughts to other matters.

It looked as if he was going to begin his

search for Devon Stafford in Mare's Nest. An obscure tidbit of news he had unearthed had mentioned she had once spent a summer on the Carolina coast as a girl. It seemed to him the romantic lure of a childhood memory would appeal to an actress. Mare's Nest may not be the most logical choice to begin with, but he didn't really have any options now.

A blown engine. His heart sank and a hard lump lodged like a rock in his throat. His beautiful Porsche.

His rescuer pulled the cab door open and hauled herself up into the driver's seat. "She's all loaded up, honey, and none the worse for wear. You can relax."

Jake sent her a sheepish smile. "I'm sorry I was such a jerk. It's just that, it's my first Porsche and —"

She held up a small hand to stem the apology. "You don't have to explain. I know all about men and their cars. Knew a fella once who had a Testarossa that threw a rod on the Ventura Freeway at rush hour. He flung himself flat on the hood and cried like a baby. It was a pitiful thing to see."

"I can imagine."

Jake studied her features a little more closely now that the initial crisis had passed. She really had a very pretty mouth, and the faint scent of a soft sweet perfume cut through the aroma of oil and stale cigar smoke that hung in the cab. Lilies of the valley. The scent drifted into the orderly storehouse of his memory to be filed away for future reference.

Dixie stared at him, unnerved by the stirring of attraction warming her tummy. Of course, he was an attractive man, big and blond and brawny. It was kind of startling to feel so drawn to him because she hadn't really thought about men in that way for a while; she hadn't had the time or the energy. She had been too busy finding herself, healing and becoming whole. This one had the most gorgeous smile — winning, dazzling. There was nothing quite like a great smile on a big handsome guy. His teeth were white and straight — perfect, like everything else about him.

Perfect. That was all the reason she needed to steer clear of him. She'd had her fill of the quest for perfection.

"You've been to California?" he asked, just to break the silence and the silky strand of sexual tension that had suddenly spun between them. He didn't have time for that kind of thing now. He had a job to do. Besides, she really wasn't his type, he reminded himself yet again. He tended to lean toward tall, slender blondes as a rule, not perky, curvy brunettes.

She dropped her head, giving all her attention to a dirty, curling log sheet on a battered clipboard. Her hair fell around the sides of her face like a veil. "Oh, sure. I've been around. I'll need your name and address for our records."

"Jake Gannon, 6868 Grafton, Santa Mara, California," he recited dutifully, watching her. "And you are?"

Her head came up, eyes round beneath the tangled fringe of her bangs.

"Dixie. Dixie La Fontaine," she said, feeling oddly trapped in the beam of his blue eyes. Her breath caught in her throat when he reached up a hand and brushed the end of her nose.

"Grease," he murmured, his gaze still holding hers as the magnetism between them soared. "You had grease on your nose."

"Oh."

She dropped her head again to stare at the log sheet, chiding herself for being a ninny. What was the matter with her, reacting to a strange man this way? A strange man from California, no less!

No, no, no, Dixie darling. If and when you go looking for a fella, he's gonna be a nice Southern good ol' boy who likes chicken-fried

26

steak and chocolate pecan pie and dances at the American Legion hall with girls who have a little meat on them.

All she had to do was look at Jake Gannon to know he probably belonged to a health club and ate muesli for breakfast and cringed at the mere mention of the word "fat" in any context. He just had that look about him, that California image. She had more important things to focus on in her life than having an image.

"Are you staying some place around here?" she asked, forcing her mind back to business. "We'll need a local phone where you can be reached."

"That's my next problem." He grinned engagingly, flashing two deep dimples. "I hadn't made plans to stay here. Is there a motel or something in Mare's Nest?"

A wry smile quirked up the right side of Dixie's mouth as she set the clipboard aside and started the tow truck. "Or something."

"Do you think I'll have any trouble getting in without a reservation?"

"Naw, don't worry about it," she drawled, resigning herself to the fact that Jake Gannon was not going to be out of sight or out of mind for a while. "I know the manager pretty good."

Two

La Fontaine. Jake turned the name over in his mind, feeling genuine excitement. Devon Stafford's mother's maiden name was La Fontaine. Maybe Dixie was a distant cousin. He glanced at her, looking for a resemblance.

"What?" she asked sharply. She pulled one hand off the steering wheel to rub her cheek. "Have I got more grease on me?"

"No, no, nothing. I was just admiring the way you handle this truck."

"Oh. Thanks."

He stretched a little, subtly altering his position so he could study her better. Everything about Devon Stafford was sharply stunning, from her cool blond tresses to the delicate bone structure of her face with its prominent cheekbones and full, pouty lips. Dixie had a much softer look. The slight fullness to her face made him think of women of a bygone era. She would have been considered a great beauty back in the days of Lillian Gish, but she was no Devon Stafford.

His gaze strayed to her mouth again, to the perfect archer's bow curve of the upper lip. It wasn't as full or blatantly sensual as Devon Stafford's, but there was a slight similarity. He leaned a little closer. She shot a suspicious look his way and Jake treated her to a charming smile, leaning ahead to catch the true slope of her nose and the angle of her chin.

Dixie's gaze darted nervously from the road to Jake Gannon, back and forth. She didn't much care for the way he was looking at her, kind of strange and familiar-like. Slowly she inched her right hand across the seat and stuck it in her purse. Swallowing down the knot of tension in her throat, she said, "If you're some kind of pervert, I'm just gonna tell you straight out — I've got a gun and I know how to use it."

Jake sat back with a surprised bark of laughter. Leaning against the door of the truck in a deceptively lazy pose, he fixed his gaze on the business end of a snub-nosed .38 pointed at his chest.

"I'm not a pervert," he declared, stunned that he'd let her get the drop on him. He stared at her in disgruntled amazement, trying to think how he might best disarm her. There were a number of methods at his disposal, but if the gun went off in the process in the close confines of the truck, someone could get hurt or the tow truck could go off the road and his Porsche could be totaled. He didn't like that thought much better than the thought of getting shot himself.

Dixie slowed the truck to a stop. They just sat there, Dixie looking at him long and hard in the gathering gloom, with Bonnie Raitt singing in the background about finding love in the nick of time. It was difficult to picture Jake Gannon as a slavering fiend. He looked completely clean-cut, well turned out in a chambray shirt and stylish pleated tan trousers. Still, she knew as well as anyone that looks could be deceiving. He regarded her with a steady gaze, and while he appeared to be completely relaxed she had the sensation of leashed power lurking under that handsome surface.

"How do I know you're not a pervert? How do I know you're telling the truth?" she asked.

"Trust me," Jake said dryly, laying his hand over his heart. "I'm a real stand-up guy. I'm an ex-Marine. I pay my taxes. I'm a registered voter."

Dixie scowled. "Ted Bundy was a Young Republican. It didn't stop him from being a serial killer." Her eyes widened and she gave a little gasp, motioning to Jake's outfit with the barrel of her pistol. "He even dressed like you!"

"Lots of guys wear chinos! They're not all homicidal maniacs." Heaven help him, he was about to be shot because he had impeccable taste in sportswear.

"I suppose they're not," Dixie admitted grudgingly. She let the nose of the .38 tilt downward. She nibbled on her lower lip in indecision as she looked Jake in the eye. "Do you swear you're not a pervert?"

Jake had to wonder at the intelligence of a woman who would accept the oath of a man she suspected of heinous crimes, but he played along with her just the same. After all, she was the one holding the gun and pointing it at a very important part of his anatomy.

"I swear," he said firmly. "I swear on my mother's life."

"Do you love your mother?"

"Yes. But not *too* much. Nothing unhealthy. Just regular love. None of that Norman Bates kind of thing. I'll give you her phone number, you can call her. And while you're mulling it over, would you mind pointing that thing elsewhere?" he said sardonically. "I think I'd rather be killed outright than shot where you're aiming right now. I'm kind of sentimental about that particular body part."

Dixie's cheeks tinted a delicate shade of rose as she sighted down the barrel of her gun. It was plain the good Lord had left no detail unattended when he'd fashioned this man. "Sorry," she mumbled, tipping the pistol a few degrees to the left of him and tearing her gaze away from his fly.

"Don't mention it," Jake said dryly. "Does this mean you believe me?"

"Well . . . I guess."

She stuck the pistol back in her purse and rested her hand on the gearshift. "I'm sorry. but a girl can't be too careful these days, you know. I mean, here I am alone on a road in a tow truck with a man from California, who I don't know from a goose. For all I know, the car breakdown could have been an elaborate ruse just to get some poor unsuspecting soul into your evil clutches."

One golden brow rose. "What a vivid imagination you have."

"Hey," she said, starting the truck and easing it forward. "I read the papers. I watch the news. The world is full of kooks and weirdos, and I don't mean to be rude, but the way I understand it, most of them come from California."

Jake choked back the urge to laugh only

because the gun was still within her reach. He wanted to ask her why, if all the kooks were in California, had everyone in California warned him about the rednecks of the South and told him to run like hell if he were to hear strains of banjo music in the hills. But it just didn't seem prudent to antagonize a woman who drove a one-ton wrecker and carried a gun in her purse, so he steered the topic toward saner, potentially profitable ground.

"I can assure you, Miss La Fontaine, I'm just a regular guy. No skeletons in my closet or basement or backyard or anyplace else for that matter. I'm a writer — a generally nonviolent profession, although it has its moments."

She hit the brakes, sending Jake skidding into the dashboard. His head smacked the windshield with a dull thud.

"You're a writer?" she asked with something like panic in her eyes. "What sort of a writer? You're not a reporter, are you?"

Jake rubbed his head, wincing, his attention torn between Dixie's extreme reaction and the little explosions of pain bursting in his head.

"No, I'm not a reporter. No need to pull the gun again," he said sardonically. "May I ask why you would care if I were one?" He held up a hand. "You don't have to answer if it's going to upset you and drive you to commit a rash act."

Maybe he really was on to something here, he thought, his heartbeat again picking up a stroke of excitement. If the tabloid hacks had been nosing around Mare's Nest, making people nervous, then he might indeed be on the right track. He was going to have to tread carefully, though. If the skittish star caught wind of someone on her trail and bolted, his hunt for her might drag on interminably.

"You have something in particular against reporters?"

"It's just that a reporter came here from Charleston a while back," Dixie said, a little hesitant, hurt furrowing her brow and tugging at the corners of her mouth. She stared out at the darkening ribbon of road and made up a tearjerker of a tale without the slightest hesitation. "He came in acting all friendly, asking folks all kinds of questions about life in Mare's Nest. Then his story came out and everybody in town bought a copy of the paper. Harper's Grocery Store never sold so many papers in one day before."

She sucked in a little breath and shook her head at the horror of it all. "That story was just pure mean. He made fun of the town and everyone and everything in it. Here we all thought he was nice guy when he was just mean, as mean as cat meat."

Jake watched, his heart wrenching with sympathy as Dixie's eyes became awash with tears and her chin gave a little quiver. She glanced at him self-consciously, sniffled and blinked. He felt an almost overwhelming urge to comfort her, to put his arms around her and protect her from the callous world. She had managed to strike a chord deep within him and bring out all his guardian male instincts. She seemed awfully sweet, if insane, and she was so sincere. Plus, she really was pretty, and she had those wonderful breasts. . . .

"I'm sorry, Mr. Gannon," she murmured, sniffing. She swiped at her damp lashes with the heel of her hand. "I didn't mean to get so overwrought. It's just that that kind of thing. . . ."

Shaking her head, she let the sentiment trail off, the silence speaking eloquently of her feelings.

"It's all right," Jake said, absently rubbing his elbow, completely enthralled by her earnest confession. "I understand."

He understood and yet he wasn't exactly coming clean with her. He didn't like keeping the truth from her, but he didn't have much choice. In view of her past experience, if he revealed his true purpose for being in Mare's Nest she was liable to pull that gun out of her handbag and shoot him dead. At least he could console himself with the knowledge that the job he had come here to do wasn't going to hurt anybody. Even after he found Devon Stafford, he realized that nothing might come of it. There was always the chance that she wouldn't want to share her story with the world, although Jake was determined to do his best to convince her otherwise.

He dug an immaculate white handkerchief out of his hip pocket and handed it to her, leaning close, the lure of her sudden fragility overpowering. He hovered protectively as she dabbed the last of her tears. When she looked up at him and smiled a tiny, embarrassed smile, he felt as if he'd been hit in the chest with a hammer.

"Thanks, mister," she whispered, her voice smoky and sensuous as she pressed the handkerchief into his hand. "It's awfully sweet of you to understand. Understanding is sure a rare quality in a man."

Jake sat back, feeling slightly dazed and amazed by the power of her charm.

"Anyway, you can see how we'd be leery,"

she said. "Folks hereabouts never did take much to strangers coming in asking all kinds of questions."

"That's kind of an unusual attitude for a tourist town, isn't it?"

"To be perfectly honest, we don't do very well in that respect," she confessed. She put the truck in gear and started once again for town. "Folks tend to like the fancier places like Myrtle Beach. We get our regulars, but that's about all."

She shot him a curious glance. "So, if you're not a reporter, what kind of a writer are you?"

"I'm a mystery writer," he said, hating the fact that the line tasted like a lie. "At least I will be as soon as I get a chance to revise my book and sell it."

"A mystery writer?" Dixie gave him a bright guileless smile. "That's great! And what do you mean 'will be'? If you're working on a book then you're a writer whether you've sold it or not, and don't let anybody tell you different. It's the effort that counts, not somebody else's idea of what you ought to be called."

Jake stared at her, a little taken aback by her homespun wisdom, and even more surprised by how it went straight to his heart, sticking in a vulnerable corner he would have preferred to ignore. He liked to think of himself as a tough professional, able to handle the ups and downs of the writing business with aplomb. The truth was, his failure to sell his manuscript had chipped the rock of his self-confidence. Dixie's words soothed that small hidden hurt.

They wheeled into Eldon's Gas and Go, and Jake's attention was diverted to other matters. His heart flopped over and fell dead into the pit of his stomach as he looked around.

The place was not what anyone would have called state of the art. At least not since the days of Harry Truman. The gas pumps were antiques, the kind with the big glass bubble on top. They bore a greater resemblance to the robots in third-rate science fiction movies from the fifties than they did to the gas pumps he was used to seeing. The garage would have given Andre a migraine. It was a dark, dirty-looking, cavernous place — a far cry from the spic-and-span environment his Porsche was used to. The walls and shelves were crammed with every imaginable kind of car part, all of them black with grease. And all of it was housed in a wood frame building that looked as if it had survived one too many hurricanes.

"Don't let appearances fool you, Mr.

Gannon," Dixie said with just the perfect edge of disappointment and censure in her voice. "Things aren't always what they seem."

Jake winced. "No, I'm sure it's a fine place," he said, not quite managing to sound convinced. "It's just that being from the city, I'm more accustomed to . . ."

"Perfection?" she queried dryly.

He thought there was a note of bitterness in her voice and he looked at her, but she was already halfway out of the truck.

She left the Porsche dangling from the back of the tow truck, saying it would be less of a temptation to anyone who might get a wild hair and try to take it for a spin. Jake suffered a cold flash at the thought, momentarily forgetting that the car wasn't capable of going anywhere anyway. He followed Dixie into the station office.

"I'll just jot a note for Eldon," she said, rummaging for paper and pen through the debris strewn across the counter. He identified pieces of mail, credit card receipts, candy wrappers, dirty rags, and spark plugs among the litter.

Jake had to jam his hands in his pockets to resist the urge to straighten things. He had had orderliness bred into him by a Marine father and a CPA mother, and was still a firm believer of "a place for everything and everything in its place." The sight of a mess the magnitude of this one tended to make him feel vaguely ill. He watched with a kind of horrified awe as Dixie finally unearthed a dirty scratch pad and a ballpoint pen that looked as if it had been chewed on by voracious rodents. With the pen held between the first and middle fingers of her left hand, she bent to compose her note.

"How long do you think it'll take him to fix it once he gets back?" Jake asked, absently noting the strange way she held the pen.

"Hard to say." She scribbled the last of her missive, signed it with a flourish, then lifted her head to give Jake a long look and a shrug. "Could take five minutes. Could take five days. Could take longer if you've blown —"

He held up a hand to cut her off. "Please, don't say it again," he said through his teeth. "I don't think I could stand to hear you say it again."

Dixie nibbled her lip. "Well . . . it could take longer. Depends on whether he has to send out for parts or not. You probably guessed Eldon don't have much call for Porsche parts. Do you have some place you need to be?"

"I have some . . . research to tend to." He

sighed and fussed with the cuffs of his shirt, then, unable to stop himself, he reached out and straightened a dusty box of chewing gum on the counter. He was essentially where he needed to be, but he wasn't going to accomplish much if he was stuck on foot. "Is there a car rental place anywhere around here?"

"Nope. Eldon might have a loaner for you, though. You'll have to talk to him. It won't be a Porsche."

Jake flashed her a smile. "I won't be fussy as long as it can take me where I want to go."

"Right," Dixie muttered under her breath as she watched him adjust the wall calendar so it hung properly. She led the way out. He'd practically broken out in hives at the sight of the station and he probably wanted to go have himself disinfected after having been inside it. The man was a perfectionist deluxe. Sure he wouldn't mind Eldon's loaner.

"I don't suppose there's a cab company around here either."

"Nope," she said. "But I'll give you a lift to the Cottages. I'm headed that way myself."

"Thanks. That'd be great." He stopped her with a hand on her shoulder as she headed toward a battered tan Bronco. "Dixie . . ."

Oh, dear, she thought. She turned to him,

feeling wobbly and strange. Jake Gannon's touch went through her like currents of electricity, sizzling down through her breasts, sapping the strength from her knees. She hadn't counted on his touching her. She hadn't figured he'd want to. But he *was*, and even though his touch was casual, it was very strongly reinforcing the fact that she found him too darned attractive.

You're in big trouble here, Dixie darling.

If he tried to kiss her, she wouldn't be able to fight him off, she thought, swaying slightly toward him. He wasn't her type and she wasn't the kind of girl who let strange men kiss her, but there was a limit to her strength. A girl could only resist just so much magnetism, and Jake Gannon had a boatload of it. She leaned into the pressure of his hand on her shoulder and tilted her face up, resigning herself to her fate and wishing she had put on a little lip gloss.

"Yes, Jake?"

"I . . . just want to thank you," he said, staring down at her upturned face with a curious light in his eyes. "I realize you're going out of your way to help me."

His attention focused on the curve of her mouth, and the jolt of attraction that hit him was as strong as anything he'd ever felt. He wanted to kiss her. He wanted to wrap his arms around her curvy body and plant a kiss on her little bow of a mouth. The way she was looking up at him made him feel overwhelmingly male and strong, yet tender. She drew out the strongest emotions in him with just a look or a word. It was amazing.

"I don't want you to think I'm just another crass city dweller," he mumbled, staring at her lips. "I really do appreciate the effort. You're a good sport."

"Oh," Dixie said flatly, her foolish hopes deflating like a pricked balloon. Her cheeks colored with embarrassment as she stepped back from him. Of course he wasn't going to kiss her. She had grease on her nose and smelled like a diesel engine. It was a wonder he'd even touched her. Not that she'd wanted him to touch her, the blasted, meticulous perfectionist.

Good sport. Criminy. That was almost as flattering as being described to a blind date as having a nice personality.

She ground her teeth and mentally argued with herself. What did she want? She couldn't have her cake and eat it, too. She didn't want the interest of a perfectionist, no matter how handsome he was, so she should be relieved that he'd called her a good sport, shouldn't she? The fact that she wasn't made her as ornery as a wet cat.

"I mean it," he went on. "Aside from pulling that gun on me, you've been very nice."

"Don't mention it," she said. "I've got a soft heart, is all."

That wasn't all about her that was soft, Jake thought as he watched her move toward his car, hips swaying, rear wiggling in her snug jeans. He shook his head as lust tightened like a knot in his groin. This wasn't like him at all. His passions were normally sane, civilized, controlled. He wasn't the type of man who got turned on just by a well-rounded behind in a tight pair of jeans. He was obviously suffering from a kind of temporary insanity induced by the loss of his car.

They stripped the Porsche of his personal possessions. Jake was careful to take charge of the box of files on Devon Stafford. It wouldn't do for Miss La Fontaine to discover the stacks of photographs and reams of notes and articles he had accumulated. Even if she wasn't related to his quarry there would still be the matter of explaining himself to Dixie and her friends — Smith and Wesson, he thought with a smile. She had a lot of spunk. He couldn't help but like that. He placed the box on the floor of the Bronco behind the passenger seat and stacked his

44

portable typewriter on top of it.

"What's left?" he called to Dixie.

"Just a couple of weights."

"I'll get those."

"No, no, I can manage," she insisted, adding under her breath, "I'm such a sport, you know."

Jake watched as she staggered across the pavement like a wind-up toy gone out of control. A dumbbell weighed down each arm, throwing her off balance in one direction and then another. She hefted the weights into the back seat, breathlessly cursing the founder of the fitness craze. The weights bounced off the hard side of a suitcase and bounded back toward her. She gave a squeal and jumped, just managing to dodge them as they plummeted to the ground. She glared at Jake to keep away and wrestled the dumbbells back inside, then slammed the door before they could leap out at her again.

"There," she said, gasping for breath, giving Jake a determined, brittle smile. "I've been meaning to pump me some iron. I feel like a new woman. Tomorrow maybe I'll bench-press a Toyota."

Jake bit back a grin. He decided to keep to himself the fact that the dumbbells were only ten-pounders. She could still get to that gun if she really wanted to.

He went around the nose of the Bronco as Dixie pulled on a battered leather bomber jacket and climbed into the driver's seat. The front seat was a disaster area, littered with junk-food wrappers, potato chip crumbs, and soda cans. An assortment of cheap bead necklaces hung from the rearview mirror and there was a Garfield doll clinging to a window by suction cups.

After sweeping debris off the passenger seat, he settled himself, but promptly bolted forward. Cautiously he reached down into the crease of the seat, and came up with a huge purple comb with long, dangerous-looking teeth. Dixie gave a little gasp of pleased surprise as she snatched it away from him.

"De— I've been looking all over for this!"

"Why? Does your Clydesdale need grooming?" Jake asked dryly.

Dixie's bob certainly didn't look as if it required a comb of that size. But a woman with long, long hair might, he thought, bubbles of excitement fizzing in his chest. He hadn't missed her little slip of the tongue, either. He was on to something; he could feel it. And pretty little Dixie La Fontaine with her charm and penchant for firearms was the key.

Three

There wasn't much to Mare's Nest and all of it needed a coat of paint. They drove slowly through the town's business district, which was comprised of one street. There were maybe half a dozen businesses, most of which had already closed for the day. The two exceptions sat across the street from each other down by the waterfront — Clem's Seafood Restaurant, Live Bait and Taxidermy Shop, and Leo's Magnolia Bar.

"Are you hungry?" Dixie asked. Supper time had come and gone as far as her stomach was concerned and it was on the verge of complaining loudly. Now that it had gotten used to a steady supply of solid food again, it had become very demanding and she saw no reason not to give in to those demands. She had suffered long enough in the name of the perfect figure. Now she had more important things to think about than getting her fanny into a size four spandex miniskirt. Things like watching the sky turn iridescent as the sun pushed its way up over

47

the Atlantic and listening to children playing on the beach.

She watched Jake eye Clem's pink neon sign warily.

"Do you think it's a good idea to eat seafood at a place that sells live bait?"

"Oh, you're okay so long as you don't order anything deep-fried."

"I don't eat fried food."

Figures, Dixie thought sourly, glancing over his gorgeous physique. She'd spotted him straight off. He was a California health nut. He probably drank bottled water from Switzerland and jogged every morning. Not her type at all. She was all through with people who were more worried about their cholesterol count than their friends.

Why then did she have to find him so doggone attractive?

"What about the little café next to the bar?"

Trulove Café had a sign so old it had gone out of fashion once and come back in. There were ruffled chintz curtains at the windows and a sign that said "Welcome," but the lights were off. "Closed," Dixie said. "They're only open for breakfast and dinner."

Jake glanced at his watch. "It's dinner time by me."

"Not around here it isn't. Dinner is at noon. Supper is at night and the Trulove sisters don't do supper. It interferes with them watching *Wheel of Fortune*. Besides, they're in their eighties. They go to bed at eight-thirty."

She turned into the unpaved lot in front of the bar and parked next to a dull red pickup that looked as if it had been rolled and then beaten with tire irons. "Leo will fix us some sandwiches. It's more than you're going to get at the Cottages."

"No room service?"

Dixie gave him a pained smile and shook her head. Room service. She wasn't going to touch that with a ten-foot pole. Her hormones had all kinds of room service in mind concerning Jake Gannon, but it was probably best not to broach the subject.

They entered the Magnolia Bar to a small chorus of "Hey, Dixie", followed by a pregnant silence, during which all eyes were momentarily glued to Jake. The bar was dimly lit and smelled of cigarette smoke and beer. The bare wooden floor was littered with peanut shells. A marlin hung over the bar — an example of Clem's fine hand at taxidermy. Three men were seated on vinyl-upholstered, chrome-legged stools at the bar; two elderly ladies occupied a small, round table near the big-screen TV. The booths along the far wall were empty.

Dixie made a general introduction as she hauled herself up onto a bar stool and motioned for Jake to do the same. "Hey, everybody, this here's Jake Gannon from California. His car broke down and he'll be here till Eldon gets it fixed."

There were general murmurs of sympathy from the men as a deodorant commercial played on TV. Dixie pointed to each person and gave Jake a name. Bubby Bristol, Joe Dell Ward, Leo Vencour, the proprietor of the establishment. The Trulove sisters, Cora May and Divine, prim Southern ladies with flowered dresses and small clouds of cotton-candy hair. They all nodded pleasantly to Jake. The instant the program came back on, however, their attention went immediately to it.

A man with buck teeth and a bad toupee was spinning the big wheel. He hit $1,500 and called for an L. The crowd at the bar shouted for him to spin again, but after some debate and a verbal prodding from Pat Sajak, the man announced he was going to solve the puzzle. This brought on groans and boos from the patrons of the Magnolia Bar.

"Guy's dumber than a red brick!"

"He left double *R*'s and triple *M*'s!"

The two white-haired ladies blew loud raspberries.

Dixie frowned at them all. "Hey, now, maybe the fella needs that fifteen hundred to get braces for his kid and he didn't dare spin again for fear he'd hit bankrupt and lose it all and his kid would have to go around looking like a big old nutria rat for the rest of his life. Y'all don't know the kind of pressures he might be under."

Halfhearted grumblings of "I guess so" came from the crowd. They all frowned, eyes downcast into their beer mugs.

Jake gave Dixie a curious look, a half-smile turning up the right side of his mouth. The sassy tow truck driving lady had a heart like a marshmallow. For some reason that idea pleased him enormously. He wanted to kiss her again. She made an annoyed face at him and thrust a plastic-coated menu into his hands.

Leo roused himself from his seat and went behind the bar to take their orders. He was a tall, lean man in his sixties with slicked back thin gray hair and a face like a bloodhound. "What'll y'all have tonight, then, folks?" he drawled, adding extra syllables to each word.

"I'll have the usual, Leo," Dixie said with a smile.

Jake glanced up from his menu with a dubious look. "Is the turkey on white bread?"

Leo beamed. "White as snow."

Jake grimaced a little, drawing a startled frown from the bartender. "Are the tomatoes organically grown?"

Leo's brow furrowed. "They're grown in the dirt if that's what you mean."

Dixie rolled her eyes. "They're grown in Macy Vencour's greenhouse and the worst thing she puts on them is stale beer."

Jake ignored her impatience and smiled squarely at Leo. "I'll have a light beer and the turkey sandwich, hold the bread, hold the mayo, thanks."

"It ain't much of a sandwich then, is it?" Leo said. He sauntered off toward the kitchen, shaking his head.

Dixie sniffed, feeling extra peeved at Jake's fussiness. She hated that particular trait and it galled her no end that she would be wildly attracted to a man who exhibited it. "I swear, you're worse than my Great-aunt Suki, and she had some kind of convoluted gallbladder problem, so she at least had an excuse."

"White bread happens to be loaded with chemical preservatives," Jake informed her. "The human body is a temple, you know."

And you worship at yours every day. Dixie bit her tongue to keep the remark from spilling out. However, she couldn't keep herself from thinking that she wouldn't mind doing a little worshiping at Jake's temple, either. She cursed herself for being both ornery and randy. The two didn't seem like a good combination.

It was Jake Gannon's fault her feelings were getting all stirred around. Since she had returned to Mare's Nest she'd been a perfectly pleasant person — once her depression and grief had subsided. Then along he'd come with his blue eyes and his blue Porsche, making her remember she was a woman and bringing reminders of a way of life that had made her miserable.

Leo returned and set a plate in front of each of them. Side by side the meals looked like a do and don't guide for good health. Jake's meal consisted of sliced turkey on a bed of lettuce and tomato. Dixie's sandwich towered alongside it — salty Virginia ham layered with bright orange cheddar cheese, all stacked between two slices of thick white bread that resembled slabs of foam rubber.

Jake frowned. "Are you really going to eat that?"

"No," she said peevishly. "I'm gonna put it in a time capsule and bury it for posterity."

He raised his hands in surrender. "Hey, it's your body."

"That's right, and I'll do with it whatever I darn well please."

"Fine, fine," he muttered, cutting his meat. "Jeez, you don't have to pull your gun on me again."

Dixie scowled at him and pushed her plate away. There was nothing like a nutritionally conscientious person to take all the fun out of eating. She chalked up another strike against Jake.

"So, Jake, what happened to the car?" Bubby Bristol asked, turning toward a new source of entertainment. On the TV screen the credits for *Wheel of Fortune* rolled over the image of Pat and Vanna waving goodbye.

"Overheated. Might be a hose," Jake said, trying to sound as if he knew something about it.

"Or the water pump," Bubby added, nodding. Bubby looked around thirty. He was built like a lumberjack and had dark eyes and dark hair so thick it looked as if a beaver pelt rested on his head.

Jake sipped his beer and nodded along in macho camaraderie. "The radiator was bone dry."

A horrified look crossed Bubby's square face. "Man, let's hope you didn't blow the engine."

"Yeah." Jake tried to force a chuckle, but it sounded more like he was choking. He stared morosely at his plate, his appetite gone.

Dixie tried to take vengeful enjoyment in the fact that Jake had gone as pale as the bread housing her killer sandwich, but she couldn't. Poor guy. He looked like a kid whose biggest, best, shiniest Christmas present had just gotten sat on by his fat aunt. She reached over and patted his hand consolingly. Little currents of magnetism buzzed up her fingers.

"I know a fella had that happen once," Joe Dell said, shoving his mug toward Leo for a refill. He adjusted the bill of a dirty red baseball cap with "Whippets" stitched across the front in gray. His mouth turned down in a frown that elongated his lean face. "Cracked the engine block, if you can believe that. The whole works just plum froze up — the drivetrain and everything. Had to sell that car for scrap."

Jake whimpered.

Dixie scowled. "Joe Dell, really! Can't you see the poor guy is upset enough as it is? We're talking about a brand new Porsche here, for pity's sake!"

The men moaned in unison, gazes falling glumly into their beer once more. In the silence the theme music from *Entertainment Tonight* gurgled merrily in the background. As the host introduced the lead story, Dixie reached for the remote control that lay on the bar. Jake beat her to it, his hand darting with the speed of a striking snake.

"This is my favorite show," he said, flashing her a smile as he punched the volume button.

On the screen the image of Devon Stafford loomed larger than life, a sultry smile lifting the corners of her famous lips, her silver-blond mane spilling all around her in sexy disarray. Then the scene cut to an exterior shot of Stafford's palatial home in the Hollywood hills. While a gardener ran around on the lawn chasing trespassers with a bamboo rake, a serious-looking *Entertainment Tonight* correspondent standing on the curb reported that on the one-year anniversary of her vanishing act, Ms. Stafford still had not been located. Reports of her working at a topless doughnut shop in Wyoming had not been substantiated. The search continued.

"Imagine that," Jake mused, lowering the volume on the set. "A beautiful, talented woman like that just flies the coop without a word to anyone. Crazy."

No one in the Magnolia Bar said a word for a long moment. Cora May Trulove had fallen asleep in her chair and was snoring softly. The refrigerator unit kicked in and hummed. Bubby cracked a peanut and dropped the shells on the floor.

"It's a cryin' shame," Bubby said, shaking his head as if the star's disappearance were a tragedy worthy of having the flag flown at half-mast.

"We're all in mourning," Joe Dell said. "Her television show was everybody's favorite here. Half the town used to come in Thursday nights to watch *Wylde Time*. Leastwise, most of the men did. Shoot, seeing Devon Stafford chase criminals was enough to raise a man from the dead."

"I know what you mean," Jake said with a grin. "I wouldn't mind getting shipwrecked on an island with her."

"Yeah, you and every other red-blooded man in the free world!"

"Those lips."

"That hair."

"Those big br—"

"Excuse me," Dixie snapped, her brows pulling into a V over stormy eyes. "I hate to rain on this testosterone festival, but I do not believe we all care to hear y'all go on and on about Devon Stafford's assets. She's just an actress, for cryin' out loud. She didn't find a cure for cancer or end world hunger or figure out a way to fold fitted sheets. Y'all make out like she's the goddess of the world. Well, I personally do not miss her all that much."

The men stared at her as if she'd said something blasphemous, except Leo, who gave her long, even look. "Now, Dixie," he drawled softly. "No need for you to get all riled up. It's only natural for the fellas to go on about Devon Stafford. She's a famous movie star, after all."

"*Just* a movie star," Dixie grumbled. "Big deal."

"We're talking about the perfect woman here," Jake said.

"Hair down to her butt and a D-cup bra. Those are your ingredients for a perfect woman?" Dixie asked. Her temper was sizzling and she knew she was in danger of losing control, but she couldn't help herself. If there was one subject that drove her right over the edge, it was perfection. It didn't help matters that the one proclaiming Devon Stafford to be the perfect woman was the first man Dixie had been attracted to in ages. If Jake thought that platinum-maned princess of the silver screen was perfect, then he was a long way from throwing himself at the feet of Dixie La Fontaine.

"And a real tiny waist," Bubby added to

the list of desirable female attributes.

"And pouty lips," Joe Dell said, nodding gravely. All the male heads bobbed up and down in agreement.

"Well, if that just don't fry my taters!" Dixie hissed. She slid down off her bar stool for the express purpose of stamping her foot, then zipped her jacket with a jerk of her wrist. "Not one word about intelligence or compassion or strength of character. This perfect woman you're describing could just as well be one of those inflatable dolls perverts order out of the back of porno magazines! Y'all should be ashamed."

"What did they do now, Dixie?" Miss Divine asked, her voice loud enough to wake the dead in the next county. It did not, however, rouse her sister from slumber.

Dixie scowled at Bubby and Joe Dell, who looked like the big lummoxes they undoubtedly were. There was speculation in Jake's eyes, and Leo looked at her from under his lashes as he dried a beer mug with a white towel.

Dixie sniffed. "They have just demonstrated that men do in fact think with a little tiny part of their anatomy that isn't even hooked up to their brains."

Miss Divine nodded and smiled pleasantly. "Boys will be boys."

"Until the day they die of old age," Dixie said with a snort. She gave Jake a flaming look and said, "Let's go, Gannon."

Jake took a last long sip of his beer, watching her intently, then he bade his new acquaintances good night with a nod of his head and followed her out.

Four

"I take it you're not a big Devon Stafford fan," Jake said evenly as Dixie slammed the Bronco into drive and hit the gas. He watched her carefully for even the slightest reaction as he braced himself with one hand on the dash. When they made a hard right debris slid along the length of the dashboard and drifted to the floor like snow. There was the briefest show of something like pain and uncertainty in her eyes, then it was gone, forced out by annoyance.

"I don't have anything against Devon Stafford."

"Except that she's the perfect woman."

"Perfection is in the eye of the beholder," she said. The Bronco pitched and bucked over the rough narrow road. "Personally, I don't believe in perfectionism. It's unrealistic."

"Not in Devon Stafford's case," Jake argued.

Dixie sniffed and shook her head. "A lot you know."

Before Jake could comment, she took the offensive and slanted him a look. "Why are you so interested in her anyway? You planning on writing about her or something?"

"Just a fan," he said. "Like most of America, I'm curious about her disappearance. Why would a big star just run off like that? Was it over money? A sex scandal? A drug problem?"

Dixie turned into the driveway of a big blue-gray beach house and pulled in front of an old garage that was full of junk. She turned off the engine and stared out the windshield.

"Maybe she just wants to be left alone," she said quietly. "Has anybody thought of that? Maybe she just wants some peace. Maybe she don't want all and sundry chasin' after her like a pack of coon hounds on huntin' night."

Jake watched the play of shadows across her face. He could sense that she was fighting to keep a shield up, maybe fighting to keep from saying too much. Her reaction certainly wasn't that of someone who was completely detached from the subject. Dixie La Fontaine knew something and he wanted to coax it out of her. More than that, he wanted her to confide in him. But he had the feeling that getting the story wasn't his only reason.

He may have come here with the intention of unlocking Devon Stafford's secrets, but he found some of that curiosity directing itself in Dixie's direction. She seemed upset and he wanted to understand why. He wanted to comfort her, not question her, but he tried to push the feeling aside.

"Do you know something the rest of us don't?" he asked, his tone soft and silky as he leaned a little closer on the excuse of gauging her response.

"No!" Dixie snapped, a little too quickly. She took a deep breath and sighed, leveling a scowl at him. "It just galls me, is all. Whose business is it why she left Hollywood? Why did people hound Greta Garbo? Why won't anyone just let Elvis be dead? Just because they're celebrities folks think they have some right to know every little thing about them. Stars are just people under all that glamour. They should be able to have secrets and private lives just like everyone else."

Jake leaned even closer, close enough to catch the faint scent of her perfume. The corners of his mouth turned up in a quizzical little smile and he lifted a finger to trace the slope of Dixie's nose. "Know a lot of stars, do you, Dixie?"

Dixie had to tilt her head back to look at him. He was too near. She could feel the power of his male aura pressing in on her, but, heaven help her, she didn't want to escape. Sexual electricity hummed around them like an overloaded power line.

"No," she whispered, just barely resisting the urge to reach up and brush back the tumble of golden hair that had spilled over his forehead. She almost forgot to breathe, he was so handsome, the look in his eyes so intense. "I know a lot of people. Just people."

Maybe he should have asked her if she knew Devon Stafford. Jake knew he could press the issue now and probably get an answer. She was off balance, rattled. But he couldn't do it. Something in her eyes touched him, something that silently begged him not to push her. He felt like a cad and a half already for deceiving her about his purpose here. It went against his code of honor to lie about anything, but he hadn't seen any way around it. Now her sermon on celebrities' rights compounded the feeling. He wanted to defend himself, but of course that was out of the question.

He wanted to tell her that his job was to uncover all the secrets of his subjects, but he didn't go in for sensationalism. He wanted to tell her that he didn't do unauthorized biographies, that every word he wrote was approved by the person he was writing about. He wanted her to know he was a man of integrity, a man to be trusted. But he was caught in a trap of his own making. By lying to her about what he was doing here he contradicted what he wanted her to believe.

He leaned back, breaking the sensual spell of her nearness, and looked out at the buildings strewn up and down the beach. Squares of butter-yellow light dotted the sides of two small cottages. The house they were in front of was much larger, its two and a half stories stacked like the layers of a wedding cake. Like the others, it perched on sturdy-looking stilts. The lower level was surrounded by a screened porch, and windows in the attic blazed with light. At the bottom of the steps that led from the ground to the front door, a weathered sign swung in the evening breeze. It read "Cottages for Rent."

There would be plenty of time to work out the little snarl about his identity and his objective. And he didn't have to force a confession out of Dixie. If she knew where Devon Stafford was hiding he would be able to get the information eventually. As he listened to the sound of the ocean washing against the shore, the urgency to finish this job drifted away. He didn't need to storm Dixie's defenses. He had all the time in the world. After all, Devon Stafford had already been gone a year. What difference would another few days make?

"Thanks for the lift," he said.

He made the mistake of glancing back at Dixie, for he was hit broadside again by the overwhelming desire to kiss her. She looked so small and sweet, swallowed up by her bomber jacket, her hazel eyes watching him warily. She looked like a woman who needed kissing.

He wasn't a man given to impulsive behavior, but there was just something about Dixie that wreaked havoc with his self-control. He leaned toward her, a roguish smile tugging at a corner of his mouth. "Thanks for everything, Dixie. You've been a real pal."

The last word hit Dixie like a rock thrown by a taunting juvenile delinquent. A pal! A pal! First she was a good sport, now she was a pal! She reared back, sucking in a deep breath, temper unleashed, ready to tell Jake Gannon exactly where he could stick his labels. Pal indeed.

But before she had a chance to cut him to shreds, his mouth settled firmly over hers and tongue-lashing suddenly took on a whole new connotation. The explosion of sensation was stunning, blocking any idea of resisting or responding. She merely experienced — the taste of him, the firmness of his lips, the sense of male power. It was a surprise attack on her senses and a darn successful one. She couldn't remember a kiss affecting her that way before. At the moment, she couldn't remember her own name.

She let herself lean into him, her hands coming up to grasp the solid muscle of his arms to steady herself. If anything, her senses reeled further off the beam. The man was a rock of masculinity. It was all she could do not to throw herself against him and beg him to have his way with her. It wasn't how she should have felt, should have conducted herself. Every warning system she had told her Jake Gannon was trouble in a great big handsome package, but the warning sirens couldn't seem to penetrate the hot haze of sudden desire.

It had been too long since she'd been held this way and too long since she'd been kissed. She couldn't even remember anyone kissing Dixie La Fontaine. There had been men before, yes, but they had never kissed the real Dixie. They had kissed an ideal of womanhood and left the woman inside alone and lonely. But Jake Gannon wasn't kissing an ideal. His lips were on hers and it felt so good she never wanted it to end.

Jake pulled back slowly, feeling as stunned as Dixie looked. Just a little kiss. That was all it was supposed to have been. A little kiss to satisfy his curiosity. But he felt a long way from satisfied. He felt charged, primed, hot. There was such a cloud of steam in his brain, for a moment he couldn't remember what he was even doing here beyond getting wild for a lady tow truck driver. He felt as if he'd been hit in the head with a brick. All because of one simple little kiss with a woman he had told himself he wasn't really attracted to.

Maybe he'd been wrong.

"You kissed me," Dixie said accusingly, lifting two fingers to touch her bottom lip.

Jake met her suspicious look with his best poker face. "Yes."

"Why?"

"Because." He wasn't about to tell her he didn't know why. A man didn't admit such things to a woman, particularly one familiar with firearms.

"That's not a reason," Dixie said irritably. So much for her moment of romantic fantasy. She had obviously just been the handy recipient of a hormonal surge. How flattering. That ranked right up there with being a pal. "Maybe you can go around California just kissing women for no good reason, but that won't wash around here. You'll get yourself punched in the nose, or worse."

Jake scowled. "Jeez, it was just a kiss. Don't make a big federal case out of it. Did I make a big deal when you pulled that cannon on me?"

"Oh, for Pete's sake, I didn't shoot it," she snapped. "It doesn't even have bullets in it. You think I'd go waving a loaded gun around? What kind of a person do you take me for?"

He arched a brow sardonically. "Is that a rhetorical question? Because if it's not I should probably plead the Fifth."

"Oh, thank you very much!"

Dixie turned and faced forward, crossing her arms over her chest, a fine red mist swimming before her narrowed eyes. "I suppose you just got all wound up thinking about Devon Stafford and since there wasn't a blond goddess handy you settled for me," she grumbled, fighting the hurt and fueling it at the same time.

Jake muttered a few choice words under his breath and shook his head. How on earth had he gotten himself into this mess? He was a calm, coolheaded, orderly person. He lived an orderly, regimented life. Two hours with Dixie had him feeling as if he'd been thrown in a clothes dryer and tumbled on heavy duty. He shook his head in disbelief.

"I'd better go check in," he said, not moving.

"I guess," Dixie mumbled, biting her lip. The jerk. The least he could have done was deny her charge.

"Do you know where I can find the manager?"

"Yep."

"Where?"

She heaved a sigh of enormous proportions. "You're lookin' at her."

Jake blinked and his brows lowered as yet another curveball came sailing his way. "But you're the tow truck driver."

"It's a small town. We tend to double up on jobs. I'm a plumber sometimes, too. You wanna make something of it?"

A little quiver of embarrassment went through her and Dixie silently cursed herself. She didn't have anything to be embarrassed about. There was nothing wrong with her driving a tow truck or unclogging drains. Those were perfectly honorable professions. It was just that she had the sudden yearning for Jake Gannon to see her as something other than the town handyman. She wanted him to look at her and see something other than a good sport and a pal with

70

grease on her nose. She wanted him to see a woman. And worse yet, she wanted him to see a desirable woman.

What was the matter with her? Hadn't she left all that behind? Hadn't she shed the need to be what other people thought of as perfect or desirable? Hadn't she sworn to just be herself, just plain old Dixie La Fontaine, to let people take her as she was or not at all?

And here she was wanting Jake Gannon to look at her and be dazzled.

Criminy. She'd known the instant she'd spotted him he'd be trouble. She just hadn't suspected how much.

"So," he said, breaking the tense silence that had filled the cab. "Have you got a vacancy for a guy with no reservation?"

"I've got a vacancy in my head," she grumbled under her breath. The last thing she needed was Adonis hanging around making her think about stupid things like clothes and makeup and counting calories. She should have called the auto club and sent him on to Myrtle Beach where he would have found an abundance of svelte nymphs in bikinis to drool over.

"What's that?" he asked.

"I said I've got one cottage left."

"I'll take it."

"Great." She shoved open the truck door

71

and slid to the ground. "Just great."

They were halfway to the steps of the big house when a pack of dogs came bounding around the corner, baying, tails wagging. Dixie promptly dropped the suitcase she was lugging and braced herself for the onslaught. Three of the four animals jumped her at once — a Labrador with three legs, a mutt that looked like a cross between a golden retriever and a cocker spaniel, and a Welsh corgi. The two bigger dogs lunged at her face enthusiastically with unerring tongues. The corgi's short legs didn't lift him as far; he settled for licking her kneecap. The fourth dog, a German shepherd as big as a pony, made a beeline for Jake.

"Look out!" Dixie yelled.

Jake barely had time to wrap his arms more tightly around his box of files before the dog barreled into him. It was like getting hit by a three-hundred-pound tackle. The blow sent him staggering across the yard. He clutched the box for all he was worth, envisioning its contents spewing across the yard, pictures of Devon Stafford floating everywhere, Dixie digging through her handbag for her gun and loose ammunition.

The dog apparently decided this was a kind of a game and began racing in circles around Jake's legs, leaping and twisting in joy, issuing deafening barks. The pair of them went dancing across the yard toward the house and Jake lunged onto the steps, heaving the box up ahead of him.

"Bad dog!" Dixie scolded, but the perpetrator had already turned tail and was bounding off toward the beach with his cohorts.

"That was a dog?" Jake asked, incredulous. He sat on the steps looking shell-shocked. "I thought Secretariat had come back from the dead."

"I'm sorry," Dixie said, biting her lip. She reached out and tried to brush dog hair off Jake's trouser leg. "That's Bob Dog. He's just a puppy. He gets a little excited. You would have stood a better chance if you'd have let go of that box. What's in there anyway? Heirloom china?" she asked, plucking at one of the flaps and trying to peer inside.

Jake yanked the box away from her curious fingers and stood up. "My manuscript. I'd rather you didn't look at it. Writers are very superstitious about people seeing their work before it's sold, you know."

"Fine." She shrugged and started up the stairs. "I always try to honor other people's superstitions."

"So where do the hounds of the Baskervilles live?" he asked. "Some place around here?"

"Yeah. Right here. They're mine."

"All of them?"

"Yep." She pulled open the door to the porch and cats leaped out, scattering in all directions like trick snakes springing out of a can.

Jake followed her into the front room, prepared for the worst. Actually, it wasn't nearly as bad as the front of the Bronco. Though the room was crowded with antique furniture, there was a clear path to walk on across the bleached wood floor. Still, the clutter was mind-boggling.

Collections of all sorts were everywhere.

A long mahogany table was the showcase for a collection of seashells. A curio cabinet was crowded with a collection of small china figurines. A coffee table was weighed down with a collection of old *Life* magazines and three albums of baseball cards. The walls were covered with memorabilia. Old tin advertising signs. Stuffed wild animals — further evidence of Clem's taxidermy, no doubt. Old hand tools, outdated sporting equipment. He felt as if he had walked into the storage room of a second-rate museum that had run out of space.

"Amazing," was all Jake could mutter.

Dixie rolled her eyes. "Don't get a rash, Gannon. You don't have to stay in here."

Jake narrowed his eyes. "Did I say anything bad?"

"A grimace is worth a thousand words of criticism," Dixie answered.

"Look, I wasn't expecting *House Beautiful*," Jake said in his own defense. "But you have to admit this is a little overwhelming at first glance."

Dixie's gaze fell on a table fashioned from elk horns and topped with a clear glass ginger jar lamp that contained a stuffed ferret. She decided to give the man a break. The house was a little odd.

"I guess you've got a point," she conceded grudgingly. "This here all belongs to Levander Wakefield. He owns the place, but I'm running things on account of he decided to spend a couple of years traveling around the world."

"You get a lot of guests here?" Jake asked as he watched Dixie dig through the rubble on an old rolltop desk.

"We get our regulars. Two, to be precise." She sifted through the junk for a key. "Sylvie Lieberman. She's a widow. Her husband was a big literary agent up in New York. Maybe you've heard of Sid Lieberman? Anyway, it's just Sylvie, who lives here year-round, and Fabiano. He's got the two cottages on the far north side because he's an artist and he doesn't want any neighbors. Having people too close disrupts his artistic flow."

Somewhere above them a loud thump sounded and echoed through the big house. Dixie's eyes went round. Jake glanced up at the ceiling, then looked at her with a perfect golden brow arched in question.

"Cats," she said. "Darn things are always getting up into the attic."

Another thump sounded, accompanied by the faint strains of pop music.

"Doing their kitty aerobics?" Jake queried dryly.

"Why don't I walk you down to your cottage?" Dixie said, striding purposefully toward the door.

Jake smiled and followed her out. She wasn't subtle, but she was determined . . . and damned cute.

Night had fallen completely now and a cool wind swept in off the ocean, rustling the long stringy grass that grew beside the path. Dixie led the way, followed by a trio of cats.

They climbed the steps to the open porch of a cottage and Dixie flipped on the light by the door. They were greeted there by the three-legged Labrador and yet another cat. This one looked as if it had once been run over and left for dead. It was black, missing an eye and big patches of fur. Its tail bent sideways at a right angle and when it meowed it sounded like a broken oboe.

Jake made a face as it rubbed up against his legs. "That's the ugliest cat I've ever seen in my life. Why would you want to keep a thing like that around?"

Dixie looked up at him as she opened the cottage door. "Because nobody else would," she said simply.

"These are all strays?" He motioned to the group of animals that had gathered at the foot of the steps to wait for their mistress.

"Strays and rejects." She leaned down and patted the Labrador's head. "Abby here lost her leg in a trap and her owner was going to put her to sleep because she wasn't good for hunting anymore. Bob Dog's people thought he was a cute puppy, but they hadn't figured on him growing up to be so big. Honey was an accident and her owners didn't want any of her litter because they weren't purebreds. Hobbit, the corgi, chewed things up. Nobody wanted any of them because they're not perfect."

"And you took them in," Jake said quietly.

"I told you." She hefted up his suitcase and swung it inside. "I'm a soft touch."

77

Jake glanced down at the motley crew of animals and gave them a rueful smile, feeling properly humbled. Dixie was a soft touch for rejects and runaways, things in need of shelter and care, things other people cast aside because of flaws. She was a nurturer, a shepherd. He wondered if she had any idea that she had just let a wolf into her flock.

The cottage was a pleasant surprise after the clutter of the big house. It was neat and spare, comprised of a kitchen and a combination living and dining area along with a separate small bedroom and bath. The furniture was an eclectic mix of yard sale bargains, but everything was clean and neat. A braided rug in shades of blue covered the wood floor in front of the tiny fireplace. Plump patchwork pillows nestled in the corners of the sofa. It was the kind of place Jake had always pictured as a writer's retreat — cozy, light, with a desk, bookshelves, and the sight of the ocean in the distance. It was the kind of place a man could hole up in and forget about the rest of the world.

Dixie led him on a whirlwind tour, pointing out essentials like the thermostat and how to flush the toilet without having it run on. She showed him the linen closet and how to open the damper on the fireplace, all with the prim, efficient tone of a real estate agent.

She was pulling back from him a little more each minute. Jake recognized the wisdom of letting her do it. He hadn't come here to get involved. His focus was on his objective. He didn't want anyone thinking he had tried to seduce his way to a story. He didn't want to lead Dixie on. And yet . . .

". . . The phone's hooked up, so you can call Eldon Monday morning and check on your baby," she said, pausing at the screen door. "If you need anything, you know where to find me. I'll help out if I can. You know, me being such a good sport and all," she added sarcastically.

Swearing under his breath, Jake closed the distance to the door in three strides. He shoved the screen door back and leaned out over the porch.

"Dixie . . ."

She turned at the top of the stairs with the one-eyed cat in her arms. The porch light cast a pale silver halo over her hair that made his breath catch for an instant.

"Thanks for taking in another stray," he said, offering her a tentative, apologetic smile.

Dixie almost laughed. Jake Gannon was no stray. Sleek and handsome, he was a purebred from the word go. It was just an insane twist of fate that he had ended up on her doorstep at this particular time of her life, after she had vowed not to pander to men who never looked beneath the surface. She gave him a halfhearted smile and turned again toward the steps.

"Dixie . . ." he said. "I kissed you because I wanted to."

Her heart stopped for one bittersweet, painful beat. He had kissed her because he wanted to. Kissed *her*, Dixie, a plain, little nobody from Mare's Nest, South Carolina, because he, beautiful, perfect Jake Gannon, had wanted to.

But he didn't really know why he'd wanted to. That question was confounding him. She could see that in his eyes, in the furrowed line of his brow, in the defensive set of his athlete's shoulders. It was a hollow victory, then, nothing to take joy in, no reason to take hope. He wasn't for her and she'd known that right off. She didn't have any business hurting now at the reminder.

Without a word she turned and walked away.

Jake bumped his forehead against the door frame as he watched Dixie go up the path toward the big house, her pack of bedraggled pets trailing after her. *I kissed you because I wanted to.* Why had he said that?

Hadn't he just told himself he didn't want to lead her on? Hadn't he told himself ten times that she wasn't for him? Hadn't he noticed that adorable wiggle when she walked?

Damn.

He hit his head again. He wasn't supposed to notice the sassy sway of well-rounded hips. He was supposed to be looking for the woman of every man's dreams — the delectable Devon Stafford.

Reluctantly, he tore his gaze away from Dixie and looked up at the attic that crowned her house, where amber light silhouetted a slim, feminine body against the shade. The body stretched one direction, then the other, moving gracefully, a fall of long hair spilling off to one side.

If that was a cat, he would eat his typewriter.

He let the screen door shut with a squeak and a bang and went across the living room to the desk, where he opened his file box. With a thoughtful frown he lifted out an eight-by-ten glossy of Devon Stafford. A shiny black dress clung to her slim body like wet silk, emphasizing her delicate slenderness. The world-famous mane of platinum hair tumbled all around her like a frozen waterfall. She pouted at the camera, her lips like ripe berries, slick and plump, an erotic contrast to the taught angular planes of her face.

She was what he had come looking for.

She was gorgeous.

She was perfect.

Jake let the photograph fall back into the box as he wondered if Devon Stafford would have taken in a dog with three legs.

Dixie lay on her bed listening to the nonsensical mumbling of the television on the next floor. David Letterman was going through his nightly top ten list. She could tell by the cadence of the voice and the timing of her cousin's bursts of raucous laughter. She scowled up at the ceiling and the noise. Sometimes she really wished she weren't such a kindhearted soul. Tonight she would have liked to have had the house to herself so she could listen to its creaking and moaning. She would have liked to have been completely alone so she could have wallowed in the sense of loneliness that was assaulting her.

She wasn't one given to fits of self-pity. She firmly believed that life was what a person made of it. For a while, what she had made of hers was a mess, but she had turned that all around. She had been so happy, so content recently. Now all that seemed to have come unraveled like a cheap sweater. The appearance of Jake Gannon in her life had disrupted her sense of calm and had resurrected needs she had conveniently forgotten.

Wild hoots of laughter sounded above her, followed by stamping. Something had evidently struck her cousin's funny bone in a big way. Unamused herself, Dixie got up off the bed. She grabbed the golf club she kept propped in the corner, climbed up on the bed and hit the ceiling a few times. Almost immediately the noise subsided.

Dixie lay back down on her belly and stared out the window. The light in Jake's cottage was on.

He was like the handsome stranger in old westerns, she thought. Riding into town unannounced, unknown, upsetting the quiet surface of the people's placid lives like a stone thrown in a pond. That was undoubtedly part of his attraction, beyond the obvious fact that he was gorgeous and radiated sex appeal like a furnace blasts heat. He was a reminder from her past, from a previous life. A reminder of the seductive allure of pretty, polished things. A reminder she didn't want.

He wouldn't be here long. He would stay a few days, until Eldon had his Porsche repaired, and then the handsome stranger would be gone and Dixie's life would settle back into the quiet routine she loved. Well, almost. She would have to have her cousin vacate the attic before things truly returned to normal, but that would happen, eventually, once Dee had settled a few things for herself.

The point was, Jake Gannon was just passing through. She had to keep her wits about her and make sure he wasn't toting her heart with him when he left.

Five

"I should live so long to see a man that good looking!" Sylvie Lieberman exclaimed, smacking Dixie on the shoulder.

They sat side by side on the wide stairs of the porch, sharing morning coffee and a view of the ocean. Jake had just jogged past, with Dixie's dogs cavorting at his heels.

In her sixties, Sylvie was trim and fashion-conscious. This morning she was decked out in a royal purple lounging outfit with a paisley silk scarf fluttering at her throat. Her small thin hands bore a load of jewelry and the spots and wrinkles of age, but her face was remarkably free of lines, thanks to her brother-in-law, a plastic surgeon from Scarsdale.

"My God, Dixie," she said. "Is he gorgeous or what? You didn't tell me he was so gorgeous!"

"He's okay," Dixie said grudgingly, absently stroking Cyclops, the one-eyed cat lounging on her lap.

"What's the matter with you? He's to die for!"

Sylvie smacked her again and Dixie's coffee spilled. "Criminy, Sylvie, you're giving me a bruise!"

Sylvie put on her wounded mother face and splayed a bejeweled hand across her chest. "Oh. I'm sorry. You completely miss that this man you've taken in is to die for, and this is *my* fault? Sometimes I don't know what's the matter with you, Dixie. I don't know what's the matter with your hormones. Maybe what you need is to see a good gynecologist."

"There's nothing the matter with my hormones," Dixie grumbled, her eyes following Jake's progress down the beach.

He had a beautiful stride. His long legs were dusted with just the right amount of golden hair. The muscled thighs and calves were displayed in all their tanned perfection by a loose-fitting pair of navy blue running shorts topped by a gray sweatshirt. Dixie couldn't keep her eyes off those magnificent athlete's legs. She watched until he and the dogs were just pin dots down at the south edge of the property.

No, there was nothing wrong with her hormones. They had been in a raging turmoil from the moment she'd met Jake Gannon. She'd crawled into bed the night before to seek the solace of sleep, but all she'd gotten were dreams of impossibly perfect men with golden hair and Robert Redford smiles. She had awakened ornery as a bear with fleas, cursing Jake Gannon and cursing herself. She'd come to Mare's Nest for peace. She'd wrestled all her demons and settled into a life of comfortable routine. She didn't care to have that routine disrupted.

"I don't need this," she muttered, glaring at Jake as he turned and headed back up the beach, dogs bouncing along around his ankles.

"Of course you need this," Sylvie said, her voice becoming gentle with understanding. "You're a lovely young woman. You need a man in your life. That's nature. Who are you to fight nature?"

"Maybe I could use a man in my life," Dixie conceded. "But not this one."

"What are you — crazy?" Sylvie asked incredulously, slapping Dixie's shoulder once again. "He's to die for!"

Dixie winced at the blow but didn't take her eyes off Jake. Jake with the wind riffling his golden hair and color accenting his high cheekbones. He was just too perfect. Perfection to die for.

The thought brought a painful rush of memories. Memories of someone who had done just that in the pursuit of perfection — died. Her dear, sweet friend who had wanted so badly to please people who cared for nothing but profit, people who believed pretty perfect girls were a dime a dozen. How easily Dixie could have killed herself in pursuit of perfection. Other people had driven her mercilessly to achieve it, not for her sake but for their own. She thought of her cousin, hiding out in the attic because she had tried just a little too hard to achieve someone else's idea of perfection. No, she didn't need a man who lived and breathed the word.

Sylvie wrapped an arm around her and gave her a sympathetic squeeze. "You can't tie everything to the past, doll. That's all behind you now. You think I don't know how you suffered? You think everyone who knows you here, everyone who loves you, doesn't know how you suffered? That's all over. Start living again, Dixie."

"I've been living," Dixie argued. "I've been living fine. I don't need some California hunk to make my life complete."

"No, but that's some nice icing to put on the cake, isn't it?" Sylvie said. Her gaze locked on Jake as he altered his route and jogged up the incline toward them.

"He's a perfectionist," Dixie hissed under

her breath as if it were a religion on par with Satanism.

"So he's got a little flaw," Sylvie said through her teeth. "Men can be trained, you know. Make an effort. You can work that out of him."

Dixie rolled her eyes. Sylvie talked as if Jake were a designer suit with a snag in the sleeve, a bargain at a Garment District discount store she should snap up and repair.

"Morning, ladies," Jake said with a grin as he came to a stop at the foot of the stairs. He stood with his hands at his waist. The dogs all flopped into an exhausted heap around his feet, but he was barely out of breath, Dixie noted with disgust.

"So are you going to introduce me to your friend or what?" Sylvie asked, elbowing her in the ribs.

"Cripes, Sylvie, you're gonna put me in the hospital," Dixie groused. Rubbing her side, she scowled from one tormentor to the other. "Sylvie Lieberman, Jake Gannon. Jake is a writer."

"Oh, really?" Sylvie beamed, displaying caps and pumping Jake's hand enthusiastically. "My Sid, God rest his soul, was an agent. What have you written, Jake? I'm thinking maybe I've read you. There's something familiar about you."

Jake's smile tightened. "Oh, I doubt it. I'm working on a mystery. Hasn't sold yet."

"Hmm . . . isn't that funny? I could have sworn there was something . . ." She let the thought trail off and rubbed her knuckles back and forth across her mouth as she pondered.

Jake turned his attention to Dixie. "I was just out for a little morning exercise. Want to come along? I see you're dressed for it."

Dixie glanced down at the old gray sweatpants and maroon hooded sweatshirt she wore. "These aren't exercise clothes. These are lounging-around-on-the-porch clothes. I don't do exercise. It's against my religion."

"Come on," Jake prodded. "It's good for you. Everybody needs to get up and get their blood going." And possibly get their tongue going about the person living in their attic, he added mentally.

Dixie sniffed, looking pointedly at Honey and Hobbit, who were doing their best dead dog impressions. Bob Dog rolled onto his back and whined. "You wore my dogs plumb out, now you want to start on me? No thanks."

Sylvie smacked her on the arm. "What's the matter with you? You've got something wrong with your legs now? You can't go for a *walk* with the man?"

It was a tempting thought. She could walk with Jake, slow him down, start on that reformation project. It was too tempting. What could be in it for her besides trouble? The satisfaction of having tried to pull a man off the perfection mill and get him to smell the roses? Maybe, but he wasn't going to be here long enough for any long-term changes.

Then that made it safe for her to try, though, didn't it, a little voice whispered in the back of her head. In the few days Jake would be here maybe she could make a small impression on him. And there wouldn't be enough time for anything catastrophic to happen to her heart, would there?

She thought of the lives she had seen ruined by that drive to attain the unattainable. Now she could do something to sway someone from that course.

She pushed herself to her feet with mixed feelings of reluctance and resolution. "I guess a walk along the beach might be nice at that. Beats the heck out of sitting here having Sylvie whup the tar out of me."

"Great." Jake grinned, turning and heading for the hard-packed sand just above the water line, his strides long and energetic. He glanced back over his shoulder at her. "Let's go!" he said, clapping his big hands together enthusiastically. "Let's get that heart rate up."

The old spirit of competition prodded Dixie to quicken her pace, but she held back, forcing Jake to slow down.

"I used to jog," she said matter-of-factly, bending over to snatch up a tiny shell. Strolling along, she examined the curl of the delicate piece, the soft polished pink of the inside. "I used to run five miles a day. Gave myself shinsplints and about ruined my knees. Walking is nicer anyway, don't you think? I never noticed all the colors in the ocean when I was running past it."

Jake looked out at the water rolling endlessly, the early morning sun streaking a river of molten gold across it, the ever-changing hues of indigo, aquamarine, slate, turquoise. It was beautiful and he guessed it wouldn't hurt to walk along and enjoy it a little bit as he tried to pry some answers out of Dixie. He leaned down and grabbed a stick of driftwood and tossed it up the beach. Abby hobbled out from under one of the cottages to go after it, tail wagging happily.

On the porch of the northernmost cottage a bare-chested man with long blond hair crouched, pointing and staring off into the distance. Jake's step faltered a little. The guy was built like an all-star wrestler and had a face that belonged on a slab of granite.

"That's Fabiano," Dixie said. "Doing his t'ai chi. He claims it's a balm to the soul."

"So I've heard. I used to know a major who swore by it."

"What about you?"

"My soul doesn't need soothing. I run out all the kinks. What about you?"

Dixie's step faltered as she looked up at Jake. There was a genuine concern in his eyes. He wasn't just asking to be polite; he really wanted to know. He studied her with those steady eyes, waiting. Maybe he wasn't just another pretty face. Maybe she hadn't been fair in labeling him as shallow, concerned only with surface appearances.

She was on the verge of giving him an answer when Fabiano spotted them. He broke his meditation, leaped off the porch and charged toward them, his long hair flying behind him, his dark eyes burning as bright as a zealot's.

Jake turned toward Dixie, ready to fling her aside and protect her. The madman coming at them loomed larger and larger. He was dressed in skintight black leather knee breeches and a wide leather belt he had undoubtedly cut from the hide of a woolly animal. He came to an abrupt stop two feet from Dixie, reaching a hand behind him like a pirate going for a knife.

Jake stepped between them, bracing his broad shoulders back, estimating how best to take the other man out without hurting him badly. Fabiano had the size advantage, which made a couple of well-placed kicks seem the best way to go. He spoke to Dixie over his shoulder in a tight voice. "Run for the house. Call 911."

Her tinkling laughter almost broke his concentration. She slipped around him, insinuating herself between the two men, and gave the hulking giant a bright smile.

"Morning, Fabiano. Don't mind Jake here. I think you kinda took him by surprise," she said. "Jake is staying for a few days."

The big man eyed Jake severely, looking for flaws, then smiled slyly at Dixie and winked, bringing bright dots of color to her cheeks.

"Is good," he said with a thick indeterminate accent. " 'Bout time."

Dixie raised up on tiptoe, trying to fix him with her most pointed look. "Was there something in particular you wanted?"

He ignored her and held out a meaty hand to Jake. "Fabiano. To meet with you is good, Jake." He tilted his big shaggy head at Dixie, grinning. "Our Dixie, she's some cookie, ya?"

Jake grinned back, extricating his hand from a grip that could have cracked stone. "Yeah."

"Men," Dixie muttered. "Is that all you ever think about? For cryin' out loud, there's more to life than sex."

"But not so much as good for you." Fabiano's expression declared the subject closed. He reached behind his back again and with a short formal bow, presented Dixie with a sand dollar. "For your collection."

She gave a little gasp and accepted the flat round sea urchin. "Oh, my, you don't find these around here."

The big man made a thoughtful face and gave a shrug that was distinctly Continental. "Sometimes we find what we do not know we are looking for, ya?"

Dixie sniffed, but leaned up and kissed his cheek just the same.

"I must return to my work now," he said. He jammed his hands at his waist and grinned again at Jake. "Jake, my new friend, you break our Dixie's heart, I will kill you, ya?"

Jake smiled back. "I'd like to see you try it."

Dixie rolled her eyes. "Criminy."

Laughing, Fabiano bid them adieu and

strode back to his cottage. Dixie gave the sand dollar a final inspection and tucked it into the pouch of her sweatshirt.

"Interesting guy," Jake said, amused and astounded, his curiosity about the artist rising now that his protective instincts had gone off red alert. "What is that accent?"

"His father is Greek and his mother is Swedish."

"An interesting combination, but then I'd say there wasn't much about him that seemed run-of-the-mill." They started up the beach again. He took a big breath of sea air and exhaled. "I thought he was going to try to tear my head off."

"He looks a little intimidating."

Jake gave her a look. "Your gun is a little intimidating. He looks like a homicidal maniac on steroids."

Dixie clucked at him in disapproval. "People aren't always what they look like. A mystery writer ought to know that."

"Maybe that's why I haven't sold the book yet," Jake said. Once again he wanted to defend himself. After all, he made a living out of delving beneath the surface and bringing to light all the different facets of human beings. But he bit his tongue. He snatched up a small stone and flung it out into the ocean. "What kind of artist is he?"

"I don't rightly know," Dixie admitted. "He's real superstitious about having folks see his work, and I respect that. I know he paints, but I haven't seen any of it. He comes here every November and leaves in May for who knows where."

"Maybe he's exploring the possibilities of excessive hair growth as an alternative medium," Jake suggested with a chuckle.

Dixie made a face at him, suppressing a giggle. "Oh, sure, you like all that hair on a woman, but on a man it's sissy."

"I wouldn't call it sissy. Not to his face, anyway."

"What a sexist you are."

Jake scowled. "I am not."

"Are so," Dixie declared. "You think women should all be skinny and top-heavy and have lots of hair. You said so."

Jake raised his hands in disbelief, looking aghast. "I never said such a thing!"

"I just described your version of the world's most perfect woman," Dixie said shrewdly, kicking herself mentally for being a masochist. "You can't deny it."

He shook a finger at her. "But I never said *all* women should look like Devon Stafford. Just that she was an ideal."

Dixie stopped and turned to face the ocean, crossing her arms beneath her breasts. "An unrealistic ideal."

"That's your opinion." Jake stood beside her, watching her closely. "I happen to believe people can improve themselves. I read somewhere that Devon Stafford works very hard to maintain her figure."

"She could afford to. She made a zillion dollars a year. And to make that money she had a trainer come in and work her like a horse three hours a day and maybe she got to eat a rice cake afterward if she did a few extra sit-ups."

Jake held himself very still. He studied Dixie's expression with a curious light in his eyes. "*Could* afford to? *Made* a zillion dollars? Why are you talking in the past tense? She's not dead."

Dixie dodged his gaze. "Well . . . no . . . of course not," she said haltingly. "But she's gone, isn't she? It's past tense if she doesn't do those things anymore."

"How do you know she doesn't do them anymore?"

"You're missing the point," she snapped, still refusing to face him. "The point is for most folks with regular jobs and regular lives and friends and families, it just plain isn't worth it to be slaves to some Hollywood version of what people should look like. I, for one, have better things to do with my time than torture myself with leg lifts. I mean, I may not have the greatest hips, but I have time to take notice of the world around me."

She moved a couple of steps down the beach and bent to retrieve a beer can that had washed in, giving Jake a clear view of those hips that curved outward like a bell from her waist. They looked just fine to him. In fact, his palms itched to cup those womanly curves. That fast, his blood went racing. One little thought of touching her and he was chomping at the bit, forgetting all about his objective in taking this little walk with her.

Rein it in, Gannon, he thought. It hasn't been that long since you've enjoyed the company of a lady. It hadn't been long at all. Willing women were not among the problems of his life. But as he looked at Dixie with the sea wind tossing her hair around her head, a pensive frown on her ripe mouth, he couldn't for the life of him recall the name of the lady he'd been seeing off and on for the past several months. Karen? No. Kelly? Tall, slim. She was undoubtedly gorgeous, but she suddenly seemed a pale example of womanhood compared to Dixie with her lush curves and plump breasts.

"I like your hair short," he said, the words finding their way out of his mouth without permission from his brain.

She looked up at him like a startled doe, as if she would have expected him to speak Latin before complimenting her. It threw her off balance, something the primal male in him took perverse pleasure in. He grinned and lifted his hand toward her short wild mane.

"It's very . . . perky."

"Perky," Dixie repeated flatly.

The man was going to drive her to violence. First she was a good sport, then she was a pal, now she was perky. Her temper simmered irrationally. Poodles were perky. Cheerleaders were perky. She didn't want Jake Gannon to look at her and see perky. She wanted him to look at her and see — what?

The question stopped her cold. What did she want Jake Gannon to see? The anorexic sylph with collagen-enhanced lips?

Shaken, she muttered a naughty word under her breath and stepped back from him, dragging her own hands through her sheared locks, as if to remind herself of who she was and why she was here. "I have to go back home," she said softly.

She turned without looking at Jake. He

was bad luck. He was a temptation that had come to test her resolve. He was too handsome to not want and wanting was something she had done too much of already. Contentment was what she had come to Mare's Nest for.

She fixed her gaze on the big old beach house and the dogs sunning themselves on the steps. Her vision had blurred and she realized with surprise that tears had sprung up in her eyes. She took a step forward but was held back. Jake's big hands closed on her upper arms, his grip strong but gentle enough to take her breath away.

"Dixie? What's wrong?" he asked, his voice soft with concern. "What did I say?"

"Nothing. I just have to get back, is all."

"Now who's in too big a hurry?" he whispered, giving in to the urge to draw her back against him — not into an embrace, just close enough so he could catch the faint scent of lilies of the valley that drifted from her skin. His hormones had decided Dixie La Fontaine was irresistible; his logical brain was not being consulted on the matter. He was losing sight of his objective, but for the moment he didn't give a damn.

His hands moved on her upper arms in a soothing motion as he murmured, "I don't

101

always know the right thing to say."

Dixie forced a laugh. "That must be inconvenient for a writer."

"You don't know the half of it."

He turned her then and looked down into her face, into eyes full of uncertainty. The wind caught at strands of her hair and whipped them across the soft curve of her cheek. Jake brushed them back, his thumb skimming the corner of her mouth, sending heat through them both.

"Will you tell me the right thing to say, Dixie?"

Answers swirled in her head. Fanciful answers, romantic answers, suggestive answers. She banned them all from being spoken. The truth was, she didn't know what to say, either. Her feelings were caught in a whirl. Yesterday her life had been as calm and safe as a reflecting pool. Today it was like the ocean, tumultuous, unpredictable, and she had the distinct feeling she was in danger of going in over her head. She found herself wanting a man she shouldn't want, thinking of things she had left behind, and yet she couldn't seem to stop the wanting.

It wasn't just sexual. Despite everything, despite their differences and despite reason, there was something about Jake Gannon she genuinely liked. The tenderness in those summer-blue eyes. The gentleness in his hands. His readiness to protect her from Fabiano. Under the golden boy exterior, beneath the perfectionistic tendencies, there was a nice man, a man worth knowing, a man worth saving, a man worth —

"I guess maybe I should have been a mime," he murmured. "I'm not half bad at showing what I mean."

In the time it took Dixie to snatch a breath Jake lowered his head and pressed his lips to hers. She leaned against him, dropping the beer can, her hands coming up to grip the sweatshirt that clung to his chest. Her head fell back, offering no resistance, inviting him to take her mouth. He tasted warm and slightly salty from the spray of the sea. He tasted like something she had craved a long time and denied herself. That it would have been safer for her to continue denying herself was a fact she paid no heed to, not when he was this close, not when he was holding her. His nearness canceled caution.

A groan rumbled in his chest beneath her hands. She answered it with a sigh, her lips parting, granting him access to her mouth. He deepened the kiss, slowly, patiently; exploring, not claiming; tasting, not devouring. It was a kiss of discovery and wonder, and when he lifted his head that wonder was reflected in his eyes.

"Wow," he murmured. "I guess it's true what they say — everybody loves a mime."

"Everybody loves a clown," Dixie corrected him, her gaze locked on his. "People throw pennies at mimes."

"Who cares," he growled, bending down toward her again.

Madness threatened to overwhelm him. He would have given his last nickel for another taste of her. If he hadn't thought Fabiano would come charging out to try to rip him limb from limb, he would have pulled her down onto the sand and made love to her right there with the surf washing over them. This kind of sudden passion wasn't like him. It was crazy and wild. It was wonderful.

As he lowered his mouth toward Dixie's waiting lips, he caught a flash of silver, a glimpse of a svelte form in the corner of his eye. Jake jerked his head up, his gaze focusing on the beach house.

"What?" Dixie asked dazedly, blinking.

Jake let go of her and took two steps toward the house, staring at it as if it had just materialized out of thin air. Dixie's knees wobbled and gave out and she sat unceremoniously on the wet sand.

"I saw —" Jake cut himself off. He had been about to bolt and run, but the elusive vision had disappeared and the distant roar of an engine indicated she would be gone entirely by the time he arrived on the scene. He wheeled around and it took him a second to realize Dixie was sitting down — and glaring at him. "I saw someone come out of your house."

"It was probably Sylvie," she said, struggling to her feet.

"Not unless Sylvie has grown three feet of platinum-blond hair since we met half an hour ago."

"There are such things as wigs, you know," Dixie grumbled, grimacing as she dusted off the seat of her pants. Wet sand clung to her fingers. The damp had already seeped through her sweatpants into her panties. It felt disgusting.

"Why would she put on a wig?" Jake demanded. "Her hair looked fine to me."

"I don't know. Why do people do what they do?" she snapped crossly. "I don't know why. She just might, is all. My great-uncle Nub used to like to cut up bleach bottles and make hats out of them. Why would anyone want to do that? Maybe Sylvie just got a wild urge to wear a wig."

He gave her a long, steady look. "And

maybe that wasn't Sylvie."

Dixie ground her teeth. Darn it all, she would have to get saddled with a mystery writer, a man who probably saw clues in his breakfast cereal, a nosy California perfectionist who wouldn't rest until he'd put everything in its place.

"I'll bet you were the kind of kid who had to take every blessed thing apart to see how it worked," she grumbled.

Jake looked down at his sneakers and snarled a little under his breath. Every machine he had ever managed to take apart had never been the same again. It wasn't something he cared to discuss.

"Would you mind giving me a lift into town?" he asked abruptly. "I need to buy some groceries."

Dixie smacked a hand against his back in a gesture of phony camaraderie that left a damp sandy print on his sweatshirt. "Why would I mind?" she said with a smile that looked more ferocious than friendly. "I'm such a sport. I wouldn't mind at all. You're a guest here. You need something, you just ask your perky pal, Dixie," she said, spitting out each *P* like a bullet.

Jake stared at her as she trudged toward the house. The lady was steamed.

Because he'd caught sight of her mystery

guest or because he'd reneged on the second kiss?

He wasn't sure which answer would please him more.

Six

He hadn't caught sight of the woman in town on Saturday. He'd kept an eye peeled as he strolled the three aisles of Harper's Grocery and as he'd followed Dixie around in the hardware store while she shopped for toggle bolts and tenpenny nails. There had been no sign of his quarry on the street or anywhere around the Cottages during the rest of the day. But that night there had been another aerobics exhibition on the other side of the shade at the attic window.

Sunday had brought similar lack of luck. Jake had turned down Dixie's rather cool offer of a ride to church, hoping the woman in the attic would emerge while she thought everyone else was gone. But such had not been the case. He ended up spending most of the day in a deck chair on the porch of his cottage, rereading his manuscript and being stared at by Dixie's array of motley cats. Fabiano had strolled over for a beer in the afternoon and met Jake's query about someone else living in Dixie's house with a blank look. All in all, it had been a pleasurable way to spend the day. He'd enjoyed the sight and sound of the sea and stretching out in a chair with his book. But it had not been very profitable as far as attaining his objective.

Dixie had avoided him all day like the plague and he had allowed her the distance. He didn't quite understand what was going on between them, either. The attraction was pulling his mind off his work, distorting his focus, and that made him uncomfortable. He had always gone after a goal with single-minded determination. Now he felt as if he were drifting in two directions at the same time.

If Dixie was hiding Devon Stafford here, then she'd had amazing success for a year. There had never been a clue in any of the tabloids. Not one person had uttered a word of suspicion about the actress hiding out along the Carolina coast. Greece had been scoured by reporters, and Mazatlán, and Monte Carlo. No one had ever mentioned Mare's Nest. Of course, Dixie had admitted Mare's Nest didn't attract many strangers. Hiding a runaway star may not have been such a difficult undertaking. Or perhaps Ms. Stafford had only just come here. For all anyone knew, the actress could have been constantly on the move, staying nowhere long enough to be found out.

Devon Stafford. He'd found her. He could feel it in his gut. The connection to the La Fontaine name, the aerobics demonstrations, the glimpse of that famous hair and figure . . . it had to be her. Why would an ordinary person go to such lengths to hide herself?

Jake had tried to further substantiate his guess by digging through his files for the names of the relatives Dixie had mentioned and for a mention of Dixie herself. But little was known about the star's early life. Her manager had decided from the outset that mystery would further her allure, so Stafford had revealed little about her background. He knew her real name — Dee Ann Montrose — and her mother's maiden name: La Fontaine. But that was about it and for that he had searched long and hard. He had found no mention of Great-Aunt Suki and her gall-bladder problems. No mention of Great-Uncle Nub and his penchant for bleach bottle hats. No mention of a curvy spitfire of a cousin named Dixie.

Dixie, who was taking her own sweet time emerging from the house. Giving her cousin a good head start, no doubt. He'd heard a car roar out of the yard half an hour before and had just caught a glimpse of silver hair whipping out the open window of a classic pink Thunderbird as it sailed down the road. He'd cursed his immobility and called Dixie for a ride. They'd agreed to meet at the Bronco by eleven. She had yet to make an appearance and it was already a quarter past. Punctuality was apparently another trait they didn't share.

Sitting in the truck, Jake thought he should be annoyed, but he couldn't find it in him. In fact, he admired Dixie's loyalty. She was determined to deny the existence of another person in her house, no matter what. If the mystery woman had fallen out of a window and landed on Jake's head, he imagined Dixie would try to cover up with a screwball explanation.

It wasn't like him at all. Since arriving in Mare's Nest he had spent more time wondering about what made Dixie tick than wondering about Devon Stafford. Wondering about the shadows that sometimes passed through Dixie's eyes, about the tears that had welled there briefly before he'd kissed her on Saturday morning. She had secrets and Jake wanted to know what they were. As always when presented with a mystery, the wheels of his mind whirred like crazy, turning over facts and clues, hunting for scraps of information and impressions he'd stored away.

All the gears were working . . . on the wrong mystery.

"This place is affecting my mind," he mumbled, shaking his head in sad amazement.

He glanced around the wasteland of the front seat to distract himself. There was a little pile of seashells on the floor, the remnants of a bag of junk food, three soda cans, and an earring. Frowning, he turned his attention to the colorful bead necklaces hanging from the rearview mirror like exotic fruit. He hefted them in his palm the way he might test a bunch of grapes for weight, rolling the smooth beads between his fingers.

Tiny printing on red beads caught his eye. There was one letter in dark ink on each bead. "2 D 4 luck J." A little heart had been drawn on the bead following the *J*.

Luck for what? Who the hell was this *J* character?

Jake would never have labeled the twist of emotion in his chest jealousy. He wasn't the type. He was practical and controlled, not given to bursts of jealousy. And jealous of what? That a woman he had just met, a woman who was his opposite in most respects, had a life outside their brief acquaintance? Absurd.

What he was feeling was impatience. He checked his watch, heaved a sigh, tapped his toe on a soda can.

At long last the door to the beach house opened and Dixie sauntered down the steps and across the yard, pausing to pat several of her dogs. Jake watched her, his heart warming at the sight of her, cute and curvy in her old jeans and a hunter green turtleneck that molded her breasts, her expression soft.

He shook his head, a wry smile lifting the corner of his mouth. "I'm falling like a ton of bricks," he muttered, amazed.

He never fell for women. He experienced attraction that gradually strengthened into something more. He established reasonable relationships with rules and bounds. He never fell. He never lost control that way. The idea that Dixie was stripping that famous control away, without even trying, irked him a little. It also excited him.

"Sorry you had to wait," she said without a hint of repentance in her voice as she settled herself behind the wheel of the Bronco. "But I had to wash my hair and I ran out of cream rinse and then Mavis Randall called and she just goes on and on, talking about her bunions and bursitis and all. There's just no end to human suffering where Mavis is concerned, I swear."

Jake let out a measured breath, schooling himself to be patient and trying not to notice the way Dixie's dark green sweater hugged her breasts. "No problem. I didn't mind the wait."

Dixie bit down on a smug smile. The heck he didn't mind. If he clenched his teeth any harder that gorgeous jaw of his was going to crack. She had dragged her feet out of pure orneriness and she probably should have been genuinely apologetic, but she wasn't. It would do him good to get off schedule every once in a while.

"You might as well get used to it anyhow," she said.

"Used to what?"

"Waiting. We have our own pace down here. The word 'hurry' never made it into the Southern vocabulary. It's not much like California."

"So far, I'd say it's not much like any place I've been on this planet," Jake said.

Dixie reserved comment and put the Bronco in gear. She kept waffling between thinking a dose of Mare's Nest would do Jake good and simply wishing him gone, reformed or not. The issue would probably be academic once he got a load of Eldon. He'd bolt for the nearest phone and call a tow truck up from Charleston to rescue his precious Porsche and then he'd be out of her hair for good.

Why did that idea bring more anxiety than relief?

Criminy, she thought, nibbling her lip. After all she'd been through, she was finally going to lose her mind — over a man.

"So, when do you think you'll have it finished?" Jake asked.

Eldon stood back from the Porsche, wiping his hands on a rag only marginally cleaner than his greasy fingers. He chewed some on the stub of his cigar, then pulled it from his mouth and spat on the floor of the garage, all the while making a series of faces that could have won him a spot on a laxative commercial. Behind him stood Junior, a misnomer if ever there was one. Junior looked like an oak tree with a face. He had a vacant look that suggested he bent tire irons over his head for recreation.

"Well," Eldon drawled, "could take a week. Mebbe two. All depends on how long it takes for that hose to get here."

Jake looked longingly at his Porsche, nestled beside a battered pickup that reeked of an active farm career. He cast a sideways glance at Eldon and thought that for the first time since he'd broken his arm at the age of eight he might actually cry in public.

Eldon was built like a fireplug, fiftyish with a friar's ring of thin red hair and eyes that were mere slits in his fleshy face. He was Pigpen grown up and gone bad. His coverall looked like something that should have been taken out and burned. He chewed some more on his cigar stub, sniffed, and spat.

Jake's first urge was to have the car hauled elsewhere, some place where the help didn't look like extras from an Alfred Hitchcock movie. But he squelched that urge. He needed to stay in Mare's Nest and it was suddenly important that he leave the car in Eldon's grimy hands.

This was a test. He could feel Dixie's eyes on him, knew that she expected him to cut and run. Blasted hormones. He was going to leave his eighty-thousand-dollar automobile in the hands of a hillbilly version of Mutt and Jeff just to impress a woman with his toughness. He could take it. Maybe Andre would swoon at the sight of this place, but he was Jake Gannon, he was an ex-Marine, he was only going to break out in a cold sweat and go weak at the knees.

"That —" Jake broke off and cleared the tightness from his throat, then continued in his usual decisive tone. "That'll be fine. No hurry. I can write here as well as anywhere."

Eldon's face took on a scowl. He pulled an enormous wrench from his pocket and slapped it against his palm. "You're a writer?"

"Yes," Jake said evenly, eyeing the wrench with amusement.

Eldon took a step closer and Junior loomed right up behind him, thick brows drawing low over unblinking eyes. Jake stood his ground with deceptive calm; a lazy, dangerous smile turned the corners of his mouth.

"It's okay, Eldon," Dixie said, pulling herself away from the Porsche. "Jake's a mystery writer, not a reporter."

Unimpressed, the mechanic grunted, his gaze riveted on Jake. "You're stayin' out to the Cottages?"

"That's right," Jake said, his voice as soft as velvet, smile never wavering.

"You give our Dixie a bad time and you're gonna be one big mystery. You got that, boy?" Eldon leaned toward Jake and tapped the wrench on Jake's breastbone for emphasis, his beady little eyes squinting into nothingness. "Junior here'll put you in so many places those prissy snots from California won't never find enough of you to take back in a lunch bucket."

Junior snarled an agreement.

Jake eyed them both indolently and

chuckled, a low menacing sound that rumbled deep in his chest. One golden brow arched and he settled his hands at the waist of his jeans. "Oh, really?"

"Eldon!" Dixie wailed. Rushing forward she snatched the tool away from him and smacked him on the arm with it. "For Pete's sake! Jake is a guest. He didn't come here to make trouble. Here he is trusting his brand-new Porsche with you and you have to go and act like something out of *Deliverance*. You ought to be ashamed." She shot a glare up at Junior. "The both of you."

Junior stepped back, his stern face melting into a look of contrition. "Shoot, Dixie, we're just looking out for you."

Dixie tilted her head and gave him a sweet smile that brought a hint of a blush to the big man's cheeks. "I'm okay," she said, affectionately rubbing his cheek with the wrench.

Jake watched her reach up and playfully tug down the bill of Junior's red Whippets cap. He could almost see her turn up the knob on that incredible charm of hers. Junior grinned shyly and shuffled his feet, and Jake felt another swell of that emotion that absolutely wasn't jealousy. *2 D 4 luck J.* J for Junior? Did he care? Did it matter to him? Of course not.

"So," he said tightly as they walked out of

the garage, just about choking on that emotion he refused to name. "You and Junior have something going on?"

"Me and Junior?" Dixie laughed and made a face at him. "No. Junior's not sweet on me. Whatever gave you that idea?"

He flashed a grin that was little more than a baring of his teeth. "Oh, just that he was practically drooling all over you."

She laughed again. "Go on. He was not. Junior's like a big brother to me."

"Big, drooling brother," Jake muttered, temper seething, control slipping. He went around to the passenger side of the Bronco and yanked the door open.

Dixie watched him with amazement. He was acting almost as if he were jealous. But of course he wasn't, she tried to tell herself. Men like Jake Gannon didn't get jealous over not-so-slender, irksome women they'd just met. It didn't happen. Not ever. It was just plain foolishness to think this one might. But her fingertips pressed against her lips, bringing back the taste of him as he'd kissed her.

"They really are top-notch mechanics, you know," she said, partly to distract herself and partly to reward Jake for leaving the Porsche. "Eldon has hands like a surgeon, only his are greasy."

"What about Junior?" Jake said irritably, flattening and stacking junk food wrappers on the dash. "What has he got besides a brain the size of a pea?"

"A degree in engineering from Georgia Tech," Dixie said smoothly. "He does freelance design work. Has accounts all over the South. Tinkering on cars is his hobby."

Jake rubbed a hand across his mouth and sighed. He let his head roll against the back of the seat, slanting Dixie a sheepish look that was so endearing it made her heart jump. "I deserved that, didn't I?"

Dixie chuckled, the light in her eyes softening. "Yep. You just about steal the prize when it comes to judging books by their cover."

"I'm the product of a very image conscious society," he said, watching her closely.

"I know," she murmured, turning to gaze out the windshield. Boy, did she know. But it wasn't Jake's fault. Society in general had become obsessively image conscious. She blamed advertising and the Devon Staffords of the world for making people have unrealistic expectations.

Pulling herself out of her reverie, she waved her hand in the direction of the garage. "That all back there was mostly an act, you know. They wouldn't hurt a flea on a hound dog, either one of them."

"I wasn't terribly concerned," Jake said softly.

"I know." She shrugged and frowned prettily. "I just wanted you to know so you wouldn't get the drop on them next time and put them into some kind of Marine choke hold."

Jake gave her a long, considering look. "First Fabiano warns me off, now these two. Saturday the guy at the hardware store followed me around with a staple gun, ready to nail me to the wall if I looked at you the wrong way. They're awfully protective of you. Why is that?"

She shrugged as if she were uncomfortable with either the idea or the question. "Shoot, I don't know. It's just their way, is all."

Jake hummed a little and leaned toward her, smiling slightly, trying to work out the puzzle that was Dixie. He knew one thing for certain — she was awfully cute when she was disgruntled. He knew something else, as well — he was falling more and more under her spell with each passing second, and fighting it less. He could actually feel himself tilting off balance, losing the firm footing he maintained in life.

"I don't think so," he murmured. "I think

it's something about you, Dixie La Fontaine. You inspire men to take up arms for you."

His smile deepened, carving out the dimples in his cheeks. Dixie had to pull her eyes away or melt. She shook her head. "I don't think Dixie La Fontaine ever inspired a man to do anything."

"Not true," Jake whispered, brushing a knuckle over the softness of her cheek. "Not true, Dixie."

She inspired him to behave in ways that amazed him. Every time he got within two feet of her, every time she turned those big hazel eyes up at him, something happened to his equilibrium and he lost all sense of balance. He lost all sense, period. There was something about her, something magnetic. Even when she wasn't trying there was an enchanting aura about her. And when she turned on the charm, as she had done minutes before with Junior, it was enough to knock a man off his feet.

"There's something about you," he murmured, almost to himself. "I like it. I like it very much."

Dixie stared into the hypnotic blue of his eyes, the air in her lungs thinning to nothingness. "If you tell me I'm swell," she whispered, leaning toward him, "I'll break your nose."

A teasing smile twitched the corners of his lips and mischief twinkled in his eyes. "Gee, Dixie, I think you're swell."

"Ooooh!"

Squinting in anger, she hauled back a fist to make good on her promise, but Jake caught it easily. He closed his big hand around her small one and pulled her into his arms in the blink of an eye. She channeled her anger into the kiss, meeting his mouth aggressively with her own.

Lips slanted against lips, teeth clashed, tongues dueled. Her anger melted into sweet steam as the dark, intoxicating taste of him filled her senses. She quieted in his arms, giving in to the deliciousness of the kiss, of being held and being wanted. She felt tiny and fragile in his embrace, as delicate as blown glass, as tender as the first spring flower. She forgot they were parked behind Eldon's garage, amid stacks of old retreads and castaway auto parts. She forgot they were in the cab of her truck, didn't even notice that she was half-sitting on a discarded burger carton. Every ounce of her focus went into kissing Jake, savoring the taste of him, marveling at his mastery of the art of the kiss. Every scrap of her attention went into absorbing the moment, the pressure of his mouth, the feel of his fingertips tracing the contour of her breast. She lost track of who she was or who she had been.

After what seemed like an eternity Jake raised his head. Just a fraction of an inch, just enough to smile into her eyes with sweetness and smug male triumph. He dragged his tongue across his lower lip and hummed. "Mmm . . . you taste good when you're steamed," he whispered.

Dixie's heart did an impossible acrobatic trick in her chest. Desire coiled like a watch spring in the pit of her belly. Out of pure self-preservation she planted her free hand on his chest and tried to shove him away. He didn't budge. He stayed where he was, showing her that he would do whatever he darn well pleased. Then he leaned back and reluctantly let go of her hand, but still held her captive with his gaze.

"There's something about you, Dixie," he murmured. "Something I've never come up against before."

That look was in his eyes again, she noted — a mix of wonder and determination, as if she were a Chinese puzzle he had every intention of solving.

"You're something special," he said.

A little fissure of fear cracked the spell. Dixie denied the charge flatly, feeling rattled and uncertain, raw, as if all her nerve endings had suddenly been exposed.

"No. No, I'm not. I'm just a woman, like every other woman," she said, looking at him with traces of hurt and anger that worked their way up from an old bruise in her soul. "There's nothing different about me. I put on my pantyhose one leg at a time, I get PMS something fierce, and I don't appreciate having my feelings jerked around by men just passing through looking for a little vacation fun."

Jake gave her a long even look. "Is that what you think I am?" he asked quietly.

"Aren't you?" she said, her voice trembling with accusation.

She cursed herself as she waited for him to defend himself or deny it. She didn't even know why she had brought it up. What difference did it make what he was doing here? She could have just played along, knowing in her heart it was just for fun, just a game. She should have just enjoyed whatever he offered, but she wasn't made that way and she was sick to death of pretending. She'd done enough pretending to last her a lifetime.

She stared at Jake, waiting for his answer, knowing she had taken a harmless flirtation and turned it into something that would no doubt hurt her. She would have no one to blame but herself.

"No."

The word cut through her self-recriminations and made her flinch. *No.* Heaven help her, that wasn't at all what she had been expecting to hear. She probably looked as stunned as if he had pulled out a rubber mallet and smacked her between the eyes.

"No?" she questioned dumbly.

"No," he said, sounding decisive and not a little offended.

"Then what's going on here, Jake?" she managed to ask.

"I'm not sure," he admitted, driving a hand through his hair, then rubbing the back of his neck. He looked vaguely puzzled. "It's not something I planned."

A little smile played across Dixie's mouth as she thought of how compulsive he was. Her gaze fell on the wrappers he'd arranged neatly on her dash. The poor orderly man. He would be thrown by anything he hadn't put on an itinerary.

"I'll bet that just bugs the bejeepers out of you."

He smiled a slow, sexy, self-deprecating smile, and Dixie felt her heart spin around like a trick pony. "Not as much as I would have expected it to," he granted, sounding surprised at himself, as if he were in the process of experiencing a great personal revelation. There was a look of near-wonder in his eyes. "Not enough to make me back off."

"Oh, my." The words fluttered out of Dixie on a fragile breath. Now what was she supposed to do? Lord have mercy, she felt as if she'd opened Pandora's box, but instead of terrible things coming out of it, Jake Gannon was, sexy and tempting. She didn't think she would be able to make herself put him back.

It had been so long since she'd indulged herself in romance. It had been forever since a man had shown that kind of an interest and not had an ulterior motive. She shivered at the thought of taking the plunge with Jake. Her heart fluttered in her breast. She was scared spitless. And excited. She didn't know what to do. She'd told herself she wasn't interested in a perfectionist like Jake, but that had been when she'd been convinced he wasn't interested anyway. Knowing he was indeed interested changed everything.

She cursed her capricious feelings. Didn't she really have more resolve than that? Did she cling to her principles only as long as they weren't challenged? She leaned over the wheel and fiddled with her keys in the ignition, her gaze darting from the windshield to Jake.

"We'd better be getting back," she mumbled at last. "I've got to take a snake to Sylvie's bathtub drain."

Sylvie Lieberman had a natural flare for the dramatic. Once upon a time she had been a chorus girl on Broadway. That was where her Sid, God rest his soul, had first seen her. He'd hung around the stage door until she'd finally wandered out with other cast members, then followed her over to Sardi's. Stricken with unprecedented shyness, he had been unable to bring himself to speak to her, but had followed her home, walking ten paces behind her all the way until she screamed for the police. Somewhere between booking and fingerprinting, they had straightened out the misunderstanding and they'd been married a month later. That had ended Sylvie's career in the theater. She had transferred her creative verve to her dinner parties.

Dixie looked around the living room-dining room of Sylvie's cottage with a smile and a warm spot in her heart. The theme of their group dinner this month was Cafe Internationale. Sylvie had spent the better part of the day decorating, draping the tables with red checked cloths, putting on display the bric-a-brac she had gathered during her world travels with Sid — African tribal masks, German beer steins, an Eiffel Tower paperweight, Staffordshire china spaniels, a small Chinese gong. Candles drooled wax down the sides of chianti bottles and yards of colorful Indian silk muted the lamplight. The centerpiece on the dining table was a Waterford vase holding a dozen miniature flags of various nations. Everyone had been instructed to bring a different course of the meal, using a recipe from a foreign cuisine.

For the first time in days Dixie felt settled. She would be in the bosom of her closest friends here. An evening with them would give her a chance to relax, to push away the tumult of feelings Jake had stirred up in her. They would soothe her and she would come away with a renewed sense of perspective.

Dwelling on that thought, she turned the corner into Sylvie's kitchen and very nearly dropped her Black Forest cake to the floor. Leaning over the stove, testing the Chinese cabbage soup, was Jake.

Sylvie spun toward her like a human tornado, a brilliant smile splitting her mouth and showing off her caps. She was swathed in a purple silk sari that fluttered with the speed of her movement.

"My God, Dixie, it's about time! I thought you would never get here!" she exclaimed, setting the cake on the counter. "It's like waiting for that schmuck from the telephone company. He might come Tuesday, he might come Wednesday. Maybe in the morning, maybe not." Not breaking her commentary, she latched on to Dixie's arm and propelled her forward. "Look who I invited, Dixie. Jake! Doesn't he look handsome tonight?"

Handsome didn't begin to cover it. Dixie stared at him, feeling strangely shy in the wake of what had happened between them that morning. Speechless for one of the few times in her life, she merely stared at him, taking in the crisply pressed dress shirt the color of café au lait, the neatly knotted paisley silk tie. Even the crease in his tan chinos was impeccable. The steam from the soup had brought out a flush of color across his high cheekbones. Handsome? Shoot, he looked good enough to sprinkle parsley on and eat.

Sylvie elbowed her in the ribs, smile still firmly in place. "Tell me, is he to die for, or what?"

Jake set the spoon down on the stove, a sexy half-smile tilting his mouth. "Now, Sylvie, all that flattery is going to go to my head," he said dryly. "In fact, I feel distinctly woozy. Maybe Dixie would like to walk out on the porch with me for a breath of cool air."

"But . . ." Dixie motioned helplessly around the kitchen.

Sylvie belted her one on the shoulder. "Go, go! You think I don't know my way around a kitchen? My Sid, God rest his soul, always said I could give lessons to the finest chefs. I think you're in a catatonic state, anyway, Dixie. What kind of help would you be? None. This kind of help I don't need. Go outside. I'll call you if a drain gets clogged."

"But — but —" Dixie stammered.

Jake took her gently by the arm and led her out onto the wide porch with Adirondack chairs and wildly flowered cushions. He positioned her in front of one and leaned casually against a post, crossing his arms and ankles.

"I thought I'd better rescue you before she knocked you out," he said, smiling softly.

Dixie didn't say anything. She knotted her hands against her stomach and looked everywhere but at Jake. She had planned for tonight to be a respite from confusion. Instead, she felt as if she had been thrust into a maelstrom. She wanted time to sort through the tangled knot of thoughts and questions in her head, but time was not siding with her.

"Sometimes lightning just strikes, you know," Jake murmured, reading her mind. With lazy grace he pushed himself away from the post and closed the distance between them.

"I know," Dixie whispered. "I just wasn't ready for it, is all."

She'd spent so much time in emotional isolation, healing old hurts, building new strength. She'd forgotten about this aspect of being a woman — attraction, courtship, the sparks and heat of desire. She wasn't sure she was ready for it.

"I didn't come here to hurt you, Dixie," Jake said. "I want you to believe that."

The poignant honesty in his blue eyes touched her in an odd way. She gave him a curious look and reached up to brush away a stray strand of golden hair that had fallen across his forehead.

"I know that," she said. "Don't mind me 'cause I'm skittish. I just think you're a little too good to be true, is all. Never had a man like you look at me twice."

"I have my doubts about that, but I can tell you I've looked. More than twice. I like what I see."

He still hadn't quite figured it out, but she

had him dazzled. It didn't matter that she wasn't tall and blond with the body of a health club goddess. She was Dixie, and she had thoroughly bewitched him.

Jake had decided to give in to it. That morning in the cluttered front of her Bronco, he'd let loose of reason and logic. Dixie was a mystery to him, but the only way he was going to figure her out was to experience her, to let go of his famous control for once and allow himself to be swept away.

There would be all kinds of trouble waiting for him downstream. He knew that. He had painted himself into a tight corner by not telling her the truth about what he was doing here. But he couldn't right that wrong now, not when she looked so vulnerable, not when she was just waiting to get hurt. He would put it off a little longer and trust that she would understand when the time came.

He took her by the hands and backed across the porch, smiling. "You look very fetching tonight, Dixie."

She giggled and shrugged. "Yeah, I clean up pretty good."

"I'll say."

He turned her in a pirouette, admiring her dress. It was a soft knit sheath in rich coffee brown and it hugged every ripe curve of her body with subtle grace that accented rather

133

than emphasized. Fitted demurely at the neck in front, it opened in a V down the back, revealing a wedge of creamy skin. On her earlobes she wore large buttons of gold-rimmed mother-of-pearl and at her neck was a simple tiny chain of gold with a small charm that caught Jake's eye and stirred a vague sense of recognition.

"That's unusual," he said, fingering the delicate golden replica of a sea star.

Dixie looked down at where his thumb was brushing her breastbone, making her heart race. "An old friend gave it to me a long time ago," she said, caught between the sweet rush of feelings Jake inspired and the sadness for a dear friend lost. "She's gone now . . . passed away."

She hated those euphemisms — passed away, passed on, expired. Jeanne was dead. But she couldn't bring herself to say the word. It was so final. Even now, more than a year later, in her heart she wanted to believe there was a way she could undo it.

"I'm sorry," Jake whispered, hurting for her, watching the pain cloud her eyes. "Will you tell me about her sometime?"

"Sometime," Dixie said with a sad smile.

She moved to stand beside him, bracing her hands against the porch railing as she watched the ocean turn indigo. The sun was setting behind them, stealing all the color from the sky. Maybe one day she would tell Jake about Jeanne Parmantel. There was something about him that made her want to tell him everything that was in her heart. But she had learned caution in a tough school, a place where everyone pretended to care but most were too wrapped up with their own success or failure to follow through. It wasn't smart to trust too easily. She knew that. Still, she wanted to trust Jake.

The sound of car doors slamming behind the cottage heralded the arrival of Leo and Macy Vencour, and Fabiano was coming down the path, his beefy arms laden with long loaves of bread and several bottles of wine.

"Looks like we're in for quite a feast tonight," Dixie said. She slanted Jake a look. "That is, those of us who aren't nutrition fanatics bent on denying ourselves some of life's greatest simple pleasures — like Black Forest cake."

"Oh, I'm not that strict," Jake said. He turned and fixed her with a gaze brimming with sensual promise. He leaned against the post again, virility humming in the air around him like electricity. "I'm a firm believer in indulging myself in pure pleasure every once in a while. Aren't you?"

Dixie looked up at him, mesmerized, like a mouse looking up at big sleek cat. She had a pretty good idea he wasn't talking about supper, but she answered him anyway, her heart hammering, her voice a reedy whisper. "Oh, yes. Hallelujah. Amen."

Seven

Jake let the photograph slip from his fingers and fall back into the box. He frowned, deep in thought, a worry line creasing his brows. Bits of memories and half-formed hunches whirled in his brain. Two and two were not adding up to four.

He stared down at the picture. Tonight, one way or another, he was going to find out about the woman in the attic. He had to settle the matter before he could proceed in any direction — with his project or with Dixie. Discreet inquiries had gotten him nothing. Dixie refused to acknowledge the woman. Fabiano had given him nothing but a blank stare when he'd asked. Sylvie had given him a bruise, smacking him soundly on the arm when he'd told her she looked great in her wig.

Waiting had gotten him nothing. The mystery lady seemed to have a sixth sense, knowing when he was watching and when he wasn't. It was almost as if she were taunting him with her nightly dance routine, then escaping in broad daylight.

And the longer he waited to discover her identity, the more confused he became. He was a man accustomed to linear thinking, but in this instance he found himself going from *A* to *B* and ending up at *X*. Nothing made sense. It was time to take action.

Pulling on a pair of black leather gloves, he flipped the light off in his cabin and slipped out the door. He melted into the moonless night in his black jeans and black sweatshirt. With a stealth and silence he had learned in the military he made his way down the path toward the beach house, where, in the attic, amber light glowed in the window. The rest of the house was in darkness.

He had seen Dixie home after dinner at Sylvie's, kissed her socks off at the door and left her staring hungrily after him as he'd walked back to his own cottage. Leaving her had been one of the hardest things he'd done. Every fiber in his body had ached to accept the invitation in her eyes, but he had steeled himself against the need. Questions had to be answered first and he meant to find the answers in the most expedient manner possible.

Dogs met him on the path, wagging their tails and snuffling for attention. First Honey, then Hobbit, then Abby. He tossed them each a dog biscuit and made his way to the garage.

Finding the ladder was the easiest part of his mission, as it turned out. He had prepared himself for a long search through the disaster area Dixie called her garage, but the aluminum extension ladder was outside, leaning conveniently against a wall, a victim of the space crunch within. Taking great care not to rattle the thing, Jake eased it up off the ground and made his way back to the side of the house.

Hobbit sniffed around his feet for another biscuit. Jake swore under his breath and dug one out of the pouch on his sweatshirt. This alerted the other two beggars and he had to pass out another round and strew the rest on the ground before he could place the ladder below the attic window.

The roar of the ocean muffled any sound he might have made. The wind had come up and thunder rumbled in accompaniment to the sounds of the waves, a portent of a coming storm. Keeping his mind on his objective and his eyes on the attic window, Jake took a deep breath and stepped on the first rung. When the ladder wobbled, he held his breath until the thing steadied, then climbed as quickly and quietly as he could. All he had to do was get to the narrow ledge, pull himself up the rest of the way, have his peek and be gone. Three more rungs and he'd be there.

"Piece of cake," he whispered.

That was the precise moment Bob Dog arrived on the scene. The big German shepherd bounded around the side of the house, barking enthusiastically. Jake winced and prayed the dog would content himself with the biscuits. But his prayer went unanswered. Bob spotted him instantly and, always ripe for adventure, reared up and planted his massive paws on the fifth rung of the ladder.

Dixie lay in her bed staring at the ceiling. Above her, Dee was howling at Letterman again. She glanced into the shadowed corner at her golf club, then discarded the idea. What difference did it make if her cousin was as loud as a troupe of clowns? Dixie had the distinct feeling she wasn't going to be getting much sleep tonight anyway.

After all that had happened today — the incident in the truck, the scene on Sylvie's porch — she had been fairly certain she wouldn't be going to bed alone tonight. She'd given Jake the green light to pursue the relationship. She'd given every indication that she wouldn't turn him down if he asked.

Of course, she hadn't come right out and said she was willing to go to bed with him. That wasn't her style. As liberated as she was, she had never been able to be sexually aggressive. She liked the idea of the man being the instigator of a physical relationship, and if that tarnished her image as a modern woman of the nineties, then that was just tough. There was something to be said for old-fashioned femininity.

"I think you must have said it a little too well tonight, Dixie darling," she muttered to herself, tossing over onto her side as frustration churned in the pit of her belly.

The way Jake had kissed her when he'd brought her home, she had wondered if they would even make it all the way to her bedroom. But then he had stepped back. The fire in his eyes had taken her breath away, and he'd kissed her again, closing the distance between them with one powerful stride, wrapping her up in his embrace as if he meant to fuse her to his big body. She had all but melted from the heat they'd generated. But then he had stepped back again. This time he had bade her good night and left.

She should have called him back, she

thought, rewriting the scene in her head. She envisioned herself calling out to him, and Jake turning slowly, the moonlight silvering his hawkish profile — of course there would be a moon; what was a romantic night scene on the beach without a moon? He would pause at the foot of the stairs and look at her with that burning intensity in his eyes. Then he would bound up the stairs two at a time and sweep her off her feet. The scene would cut to her moonlit bedroom, the two of them naked, sheets twisting around them, passion scenting the air as they made wild love.

Turning onto her other side, she smacked her pillow with a fist. Too bad she wasn't as good at seduction in real life as she was in her imagination. Then maybe she would be making a little noise of her own in this room instead of listening to her cousin's television through the ceiling.

A scrape and a bang sounded somewhere outside her window. Scrape, bang. Scrape, bang. Bob Dog barking in rhythm.

"Must be a shutter loose," she mumbled, making a mental note to fix it the next day. She would have to make a run to the hardware store first, though, and buy a decent ladder.

Scrape, bang. Scrape, bang. Then there

was a loud clattering, and the unmistakable sound of a human cry.

Dixie's blood ran cold. Bounding out of her bed, she shoved her arms into her flowered kimono and belted it hastily. She grabbed her golf club and dashed to the window, visions of cat burglars dancing in her head. What should she do? Call the sheriff? Alert Dee? Scream and hope Fabiano heard her?

She peered out the window, seeing nothing at first. Then she spied a human form.

"Jake!"

She threw open the window and screen and stuck her head out into the cool night air. Jake clung by his fingertips to the narrow ledge below her window, his body hugging the sloping roof of the first floor of the house. On the ground, the dogs milled around, looking up at him, barking. Bob Dog bounded up and down the length of the fallen ladder in excitement.

"What the Sam Hill are you doing hanging from my roof?" Dixie demanded, snagging a handful of hair back from her eyes.

"Trying to keep from falling to my death," Jake said, adjusting his hold on the ledge.

"I can see that. What happened?"

"Your brainless brute of a dog tried to climb the ladder with me," he growled, his temper worsening as his arms began to tire.

Dixie frowned. "Now, don't go blaming Bob Dog. He's just a puppy and he likes you something fierce, Jake. He didn't mean any harm. What were you doing on that ladder in the first place?"

Jake glared up at her, his expression the picture of frustration. "Dixie, do you mind if we discuss this at a more convenient time? I'm sure I'll feel more sociable once I get my feet on solid ground again. The threat of becoming a quadriplegic tends to ruin my natural gift for conversation."

"Well, you don't have to get snippy. Hang on."

"I'm not going anywhere if I can help it."

Dixie pulled back inside the room and flipped on a lamp. Going to the foot of her big brass bed, she knelt and dug around under the ruffled bed skirt. Her fingers closed around a coil of rope, the end of which was tied securely around the bedpost. She'd fastened it there in the event the house ever caught fire and she needed to escape, but this emergency seemed just as appropriate.

"Here you go," she said, tossing the coil out the window. The rope fluttered out into space, unfurling and inciting the dogs to another barking riot.

Jake grabbed the lifeline, and pulled himself up enough to get a toehold on the shingles, then started up the incline toward Dixie's window. She reached for him and yanked with all her might. He stumbled over the sill and grabbed for Dixie instinctively to keep from falling, and together they tumbled across the unmade bed.

"Well." Jake put on his most winning smile and raised himself up on one elbow to look down at Dixie. "That didn't go quite the way I'd planned it."

"You — you planned . . . ?" she stammered, confusion pulling her brows together.

She stared up at him, her heart hammering. He was impossibly handsome. The lamplight turned his hair the color of burnished brass. He looked rugged and tough and terribly male leaning over her. Yet ten seconds ago he had been dangling from her roof.

Tears flooded her eyes and a fist of dread tightened in her chest. He could have been killed. He'd scaled the side of her house to surprise her and had nearly gotten himself killed in the process.

"You fool!" she shouted, her belated terror unleashing itself in the form of anger. Her right hand groped for a neck roll pillow and she smacked Jake soundly on the head with it.

"Ouch!" he exclaimed, pressing a hand to his ear.

Dixie rolled out from beneath him and shot up off the bed. She grabbed her 2-iron and brandished it like a baseball bat.

"You could have been killed! Do you know that? You could have fallen and broken your stupid neck!" She took a halfhearted swipe at him with the club. "Who do you think you are — Errol Flynn swinging around on rooftops? You could have been killed!"

Sitting up on the bed, Jake leaned back to dodge a second swing of the club. "Well, I wasn't — but I have a feeling you're bent on rectifying the situation."

Dixie sniffed as the tears began to come in earnest. Aftershocks shuddered through her, and her strength flagged. This time when she swept the golf club in Jake's direction, he caught it by the shaft. In the blink of an eye he was on his feet and had Dixie in his arms. The club dropped harmlessly to the floor.

Dixie fell against his chest gladly, crying into his sweatshirt. She burrowed against him, seeking out his solid strength, his masculine warmth, trying to calm herself with the reality of him. He was safe. He was here.

"Hey," he whispered, burying a hand in the wild curls of her chestnut mane. "What

146

happened to that cool-headed lady who was interrogating me while I was hanging from that ledge?"

"She's crying all over your shirt," she mumbled. She wrapped her arms around his lean hard waist in a fierce grip. "You scared the living daylights out of me."

"I'm sorry," he murmured, bending down to press a kiss to the top of her head. He rubbed his cheek against the silk of her hair and breathed in the scent of lilies of the valley. She was crying because she'd been afraid for him, because she cared for him. That idea warmed him like nothing ever had. He hugged her a little tighter and kissed her ear. "I never meant to scare you, sweetheart. It was supposed to be a surprise."

What the hell? he thought as he rocked her in his arms. If he had to make something up, why not this? It wasn't as if he hadn't wanted to be in Dixie's bedroom all along, anyway.

"I was surprised all right. I thought you were a cat burglar. You're just lucky I left my gun in the truck."

"Yeah. I thought it would have been embarrassing enough explaining falling off the roof. Having you shoot me would have topped that, I guess."

A chuckle escaped Dixie as she tipped her head back and looked up at him. "Were you really climbing up here just to surprise me?"

His smile tightened a fraction. "Can you think of a better reason?"

"I swear, I can't think at all since I met you," she said, shaking her head. "I didn't have you pegged for a romantic adventurer, though."

Jake clicked his tongue and gave her a look of mock disappointment. "You shouldn't have had me pegged at all, Dixie. You shouldn't go around trying to pin labels on people."

One corner of her mouth lifted in a smile. "Touché."

He brushed her tears away with his thumbs and gave her a tender look. "All done crying?" At her nod he gave her a wicked grin. "Good, because I can think of lots better things to do with our time."

He pulled her down to the bed, falling once again on the tangled floral sheets and fluffy comforter. He slanted his mouth across hers in a kiss brimming with sweet passion, and the power of the attraction that sizzled between them burned away his determination to settle questions first. With Dixie warm and willing in his arms he couldn't think why it mattered who or where Devon Stafford was. Dixie was the mystery he wanted to explore — slowly and intimately.

Dixie arched up against him. She tangled her hands in his hair, loving the feel of the silky strands between her fingers, loving the velvety texture of his tongue as it slid against hers. He tasted dark and rich and the feel of him against her was heaven.

She swept her hands across his broad shoulders and down his back, tugging the hem of his sweatshirt up, baring smooth hard flesh with each inch. He broke the kiss long enough to discard his gloves, then the shirt, yanking it over his head and flinging it across the room.

Dixie grinned. "Aren't you gonna go fold that properly and put it in its place?"

"I'm more interested in putting you in your place," he said, leaning over her, his voice a low purr that set all her nerve ends humming.

Her gaze drifted down from the mischief in his eyes to the muscles of his shoulders and chest. He was beautifully sculpted, perfectly proportioned, his tan skin dusted with a scattering of golden hair. She splayed the fingers of one hand over his breastbone and felt the strong pulsing of his heart.

"And where's my place?" she asked breathlessly, lifting her eyes to meet his again.

"Beneath me," he murmured, lowering himself to kiss her. "Around me, tight, hot."

"Oh, my," Dixie whispered as he pressed himself intimately against her. A low groan escaped her at the delicious sensation of his weight settling over her and at the erotic feel of his maleness straining against her. Already she could imagine the way he would feel inside her — full and throbbing deep within her.

"Oh, my, yes," she whispered, stroking her hands down his back and lifting her hips to meet his.

"I want you, Dixie," Jake growled against her throat. "I've wanted you from the first."

"You've got me, sugar," she murmured seductively, tracing a fingernail down the back of his neck. "Make the most of it."

The last tiny shred of sanity slipped from Jake's grasp. His original mission was entirely forgotten. All he could think of now was Dixie. He couldn't get enough of the taste of her or the feel of her soft curves pressing into the hard contours of his body. As with every other time he had gotten too close to her, the electric essence of what made her Dixie completely wiped out his brain's capacity to reason. There was no logic in this, only heat and magic and a desire that seared the very core of him. The attraction that had hummed between them from the first overpowered everything else.

He dragged his mouth from hers and moved downward, murmuring his pleasure as she arched her neck for him. He nibbled kisses along the ivory column, tracing the way first with his fingertips. He lingered at the hollow at the base of her throat, drawing the tip of his tongue over the V of her collarbone and dipping into the shallow well above it. He could feel her pulse there, throbbing, racing, pounding as wildly as his own.

He slid his hand down her robe over her breast. The silk was cool and smooth beneath his palm, the globe beneath it full and ripe. Her nipple hardened to a bead and she gasped as he rubbed the silk fabric over it. Slowly he bent his head and pressed his tongue against the raised pebble of flesh, wringing another gasp from her. He wet the fabric, then blew gently on it. Dixie shuddered beneath him.

Raising up on one arm, he traced the tips of his fingers over the robe to the sash that belted it. With excruciating slowness he untied the wide ribbon until the two sides of the garment slid apart several inches, revealing her nakedness.

Jake trailed a forefinger along her ribs, which rose and fell with each shallow breath. With that same finger he drew the left side of the robe away from her, unveiling more of her body.

She was everything a woman was meant to be. All creamy skin and soft womanly contours. Amber light and shadows emphasized the planes and hollows and slopes. The curve of her hip was a graceful flare, indenting at her small waist. Her breast was large, round and heavy, swollen. Its peak pouted for his attention, the large areola a perfect circle of dusky brown. And below, where her breast met her rib cage, was a —

Jake's heart jolted as his gaze fastened intently on the small tattoo. It wouldn't have been noticeable had she not been on her back; the plumpness of her breast would have hidden it. But there it was — a tiny butterfly. The detail was impeccable, the colors exquisite — saffron and sapphire and fuchsia and emerald.

It was beautiful. It was unique. It was Devon Stafford's. There was no doubt in his mind. The subtle suspicions and hunches rushed to the surface of his mind like air bubbled from the murky depths of his subconscious. The sea star necklace, the lily-of-the-valley perfume, the odd way she held a pen, the angular look of her face as they'd stood in the shadow of the gas pumps at Eldon's. *Understanding is such a rare quality in a man.* That was a line right out of *Full Moon Fever.* She'd used it on him the night they'd met. She'd dazed him with it and with the power of her charm. Now the tattoo. It was irrefutable evidence.

Dixie. His curvy down-home Dixie was Devon Stafford, runaway glamour girl, sex symbol of the decade.

He looked at her now, at the cropped-off brown curls and the soft fullness of her face. She was watching him with her big hazel eyes full of expectation and uncertainty. She didn't look anything like the woman who had taken Hollywood by storm. Gone were the long silver-blond locks, the slender body of the health club goddess. The vibrant, emerald green eyes? Contact lenses, of course. The sultry exaggerated pout? Probably collagen injections that had long since worn off. The idol had vanished. All this time she'd been hiding in plain sight, disguised as her real self.

"What's wrong?" she asked, the tremor in her voice betraying her fear that he found her lacking.

"Nothing," he whispered. "Nothing."

Nothing except that he'd been a fool.

He'd done exactly what Dixie had accused him of more than once — judged by appearances. She didn't look like the woman on the screen, so he had discounted the clues and ignored his hunches. What he had failed to remember was that the woman on the big screen didn't really exist. Devon Stafford was a creation of Hollywood and they weren't in Hollywood anymore.

A hundred thoughts whirled through his head. Theories, questions — oh, the questions! Why had she left? What had gone wrong? Who was the friend she had lost? But he shut them all out as Dixie raised herself up on her elbows and looked at him, her eyes brimming with tears.

"Jake?" she asked, her voice as thin as a thread. "Don't you . . . don't you want me?"

His heart melted at her question and her expression. It didn't mater who she had been. Right now she was a woman doubting herself. She was vulnerable and sweet and he was falling in love with her. Falling in love — not with Devon Stafford, the ideal woman, but with Dixie La Fontaine, sweet uncertain Dixie with the big heart and the shadows in her eyes.

"I want you more than I want air," he said, and it was the truth. His body ached to join hers. "I want you so bad it hurts."

"Then let's do something about it."

Dixie sat up slowly, pushing Jake back onto his haunches. Her robe slid down off one shoulder. She ignored it, her attention riveted on him.

For a minute there she'd been terrified she'd lost him, just as sure as if he'd fallen off the roof. Insecurities had clogged her throat and flooded her eyes. She liked herself just fine the way she was — full-bodied, curvy — but Jake was a perfectionist and his idea of feminine perfection was a blond wraith, a rail-thin creature with tumbling long hair and pouting lips, a woman who no longer existed in the real world.

For just a second she'd almost wished herself . . . no. She couldn't be Devon Stafford again, not for Jake, not for anybody. She was Dixie La Fontaine and Jake Gannon would have to love her as she was or not at all.

He muttered a few words in a tone of adoration that broke through her misgivings. He raised his hands to cup her breasts, to lift them and knead them with his long strong fingers. He leaned down to bury his face between them as he rubbed her nipples with his thumbs. A shower of sensual sparks rained through her, drowning her in feeling and desire.

When he sat back again she leaned forward to kiss his chest. She pressed her lips to the skin above his heart, drinking in the warm taste of him. She let her hands roam over him, memorizing each line and slope of muscle. She teased his flat brown nipples the way he had hers, then flicked her tongue across each tight nub, chuckling wickedly at the shudder that passed through his big body.

Hungrily she watched the shiver that rippled the washboard surface of his stomach and disappeared beneath the waistband of his jeans, and she trailed the fingers of one hand after it, as if she might be able to find it again and capture it. Jake sucked in a breath as she dipped two fingers inside his pants and deftly popped the metal button from its mooring. She eased the zipper down one inch at a time, the sound of it seeming loud enough to fill the room. The denim parted, revealing snow white briefs that strained to contain him. Dixie cupped her hand gently over the end of his shaft, and Jake groaned and swore and struggled for air.

He rocked away from her and twisted off the bed. The jeans and briefs came off in one big knot that was flung aside. He turned back toward her, naked and magnificent, a predatory gleam in his eyes.

"Now let's talk about putting things in

their proper places," he said with silky, sexy menace, drawing an excited giggle from Dixie.

He pounced back onto the bed and Dixie squealed and laughed and squirmed as he lowered his body over hers and pressed her into the mattress. She gasped and moaned as he slid down her body, pressing his belly against her feminine mound, catching the thrusting peak of her breast in his mouth.

He sucked at her hungrily, greedily, one breast, then the other, tormenting her nipples with his lips and his tongue as his hand moved to torment her elsewhere. Shifting his weight to the side, he slid his fingers through the nest of dark curls covering her femininity and probed the warm cleft between her thighs. She raised her hips off the bed in invitation, but he only teased her, touching, stroking, never satisfying, yet stoking the fire that burned within her until she thought it would consume her in one wild burst of flame. All the while his mouth tugged at her breast, sending shock waves of pleasure shooting through her to twist into the core of her desire.

She begged him shamelessly, but her pleas fell on deaf ears. He seemed bent on driving her stark raving mad. She could feel herself rushing toward that precipice and would have gratefully hurled herself off, but he pulled away at the last second and her sanity came to a screeching halt.

He kneeled between her thighs, watching her face, his own expression taut with desire.

"I hate to bring this up now," he said, panting for air. "But I'm afraid I'm not exactly fully prepared."

"You look fine to me, honey," Dixie said with a heartfelt groan, eating him up with her eyes. She reached out to stroke him, finding him as hard and smooth as marble, yet hot and pulsing.

"I meant protection-wise," he said through his teeth.

"Oh. Oh, no." She looked glum as she pulled her hand back. Then she brightened. "Wait. Wait," she said, scrambling off the bed, her robe falling off her completely as she raced to the big cherry dresser along the wall.

She tried like mad to remember where she'd put the package. She was sure she'd brought it up here, unable to throw anything away but equally unable to face the embarrassment of having her cousin find it. She pulled open a drawer, flung a bra and a pair of pantyhose over her shoulder, then squealed with delight as she came up with her prize.

"You found the Holy Grail?" Jake asked, propping himself against the mountain of frilly pillows along the ornate brass headboard of the bed.

"A million times better," Dixie said, hopping onto the mattress. She snuggled up to him and dangled an envelope in front of him. "Free samples. They came in the mail."

Jake examined the contents of the envelope as Dixie set herself to the task of exploring his body with her hands and mouth.

" 'At last protection can be playful and fun,' " he read aloud. " 'Perky bright colors and patterns add a zany touch to practicality.' "

"Jake, honey," Dixie said, nibbling his belly. "I mean for you to use them, not read them. You're breaking the mood here, sugar."

"I doubt much of anything could break the mood quite like a candy-striped condom," he said dryly, then Dixie dropped her head a little lower and his whole body went as tight as a bowstring. "On the other hand, I'm always willing to try new things."

Dixie stretched a leg over the edge of the bed and yanked the cord of the lamp out of the socket with her toes. Jake pulled her up into his embrace and rolled her beneath him, tangling them both in the sheets.

He eased into the heat of her slowly, savoring the union and fighting for control all at once.

Dixie sighed at the exquisite sense of being filled with him. Again she lifted her hips in invitation, accepting all he had to give her, taking him deep and hanging on for dear life.

She'd never wanted anything as badly as she wanted Jake Gannon to love her — with his body, with his heart. It had all happened so fast it had made her head spin, but there was no denying it. She was falling in love with him and nothing had ever seemed as right as this. And Lord have mercy, nothing had ever felt as good!

The passion exploded around them like a cloudburst, sweeping away all thought and all control. Jake drove into her, the elemental need to brand her as his own driving him beyond finesse and self-discipline. He was dimly aware that this was the first time he'd ever lost all restraint with a woman and that awareness left him with a feeling of awe and wonder. But those sensations were overrun by others — Dixie, hot and tight around him; Dixie with tears in her eyes as she'd wondered aloud if he wanted her. Wanted her? Hell, he wanted to consume her, he wanted to lose himself in her, never to be found again. She was sweet wild heaven beneath him, giving herself without reserve, taking him with unrestrained joy. She called out his name and cried out her pleasure and arched up against him for more.

Dixie met his every thrust, straining into him, her hands clutching at his back and hips. She felt free, jubilant, on the verge of bursting into a million brilliant shards. The attraction that had buzzed between them from the moment they first met had frightened her and she had fought against it, but now she gave herself over to it and the thrill of surrender was incredible.

The old brass bed rocked and thumped and banged against the wall, shuddering and creaking under the onslaught of desire unleashed. A lamp tipped over on the nightstand, knocking a stack of books to the floor. But the storm raged on, unabated. Jake groaned and gasped out urgent words, pleas, commands. Dixie answered him with a chant that rose to a window-shaking crescendo as he drove into her in one last powerful thrust. The explosion stole what was left of her breath and Dixie felt her consciousness dim as kaleidoscopic colors swirled in her head. She clung to Jake with arms and legs, anchoring herself to him as the world spun crazily around her.

Her moans of ecstasy ebbed, until she was

merely panting. An incredible laziness stole through her body and she felt herself sink deeper into the mattress. She opened her eyes and smiled up at Jake.

"Oh, my," she whispered.

He smiled a secretive lover's smile. "You took the words right out of my mouth."

He leaned down to kiss her again, but a thumping on the ceiling brought him up short. He turned onto his side, propped himself up on one elbow and cast a curious look upward.

There was another series of thumps, followed by an angry female voice shouting down through the plaster. "Hold it down, for crying out loud! Some people are trying to sleep, you know."

Dixie felt herself turning pink clear to her toes. She pressed a hand to her mouth to suppress an embarrassed giggle. Jake slanted her a look, raising one eyebrow.

"Dixie, honey," he said calmly. "Who's living in your attic?"

Eight

"You have to swear you won't tell a soul. On your honor as a former Marine," Dixie said solemnly. She scooted up and nestled against the mound of pillows, tugging the sheet with her and tucking it demurely under her arms. She looked at Jake expectantly.

He rolled his eyes. "Dixie —"

"I mean it, Jake. I saw sworn to secrecy and already I'm in trouble. You have to swear."

"Okay, I swear," he said, sitting up beside her. He leaned over and righted the lamp on the bedside table and turned it on. A little puddle of amber light spilled down from under the ruffled shade, leaving most of the room in shadow. The faintest part of the light cast itself over Dixie's sober features.

"On your honor?" she said.

Jake sighed. "On my honor. Now, are you going to tell me or do I have to run up there buck naked and see for myself?"

Dixie gasped and pinched his belly. "Don't you dare! If you think I'm sharing you, you can just think again, Jake Gannon. I know you're from California where people are into all sorts of kinky stuff, but I don't go in for that kind of thing. I'm an old-fashioned girl, mostly —"

"Dixie!" Jake laughed in exasperation. "Tell me. Now. Before I grow old and die. Who is living in your attic?"

She took a deep breath and sighed, resigning herself to telling the tale. "It's my cousin Dee from Myrtle Beach. Delia La Fontaine. She's hiding in my attic on account of her fiancé, Tyler Holt."

"Was he abusing her? Why didn't she go to the police?"

"Oh, no, it's nothing like that. I mean, Tyler talks pretty tough sometimes, but he wouldn't really hurt her. The thing is, Delia had this long, long blond hair and it was pretty enough on its own, but Tyler used to go on and on about how he wished it were more silvery and thick and wavy, how sexy it would be and how it would be just like —" She broke off and swallowed down the rest of that sentence, not caring to remind herself of her own unwitting role in the tragedy.

"Anyway, Dee got it into her head that she had to look whatever way Tyler thought was perfect, so she went on in to Miss Earlene's College of Cosmetology and had her hair bleached and permed, and I don't know if it was the combination of chemicals or what, but all her pretty blond hair just broke right off at the roots. Now she's plumb scared to death to let Tyler see her for fear he'll think she's so ugly he'll ask for his ring back."

Jake's broad shoulders began to shake as he struggled to keep his laughter locked in his chest. He tightened his lips and turned nearly purple, but lost the battle. As he brought a hand up to try to smother his chuckles, Dixie grabbed one of her trusty neck roll pillows and belted him with it.

"Don't you dare laugh! This isn't a bit funny. How would you like it if all your hair broke off?"

"I'd look like a Marine," Jake said, sputtering. "Does she?"

Dixie smacked him again with her pillow as he doubled over laughing. She narrowed her eyes at him. "You're just mean, that's what you are. Here my poor cousin is, living in fear of rejection from the man she loves and you're just sittin' here laughin' like a big old donkey!"

"I'm sorry," Jake said, gasping for air. He schooled his features into a look that was as close to contrition as he could get under the circumstances. "Really, honey, I'm sorry. It's just . . . a pretty odd story, you have to admit."

"It's a tragedy, is what it is," Dixie said glumly. She could only wonder how many other women were sitting around the world miserable because they couldn't get themselves to look like Devon Stafford.

Jake nodded slowly, sobering as he took in Dixie's expression, and thought about things she'd said over the past few days. He saw the whole picture with more clarity than Dixie could have realized. Tyler Holt was one of the many who had cast Devon Stafford in the role of the perfect woman, and Dixie, who so disliked the idea of the perfect image, blamed herself for what had happened. Through means he could only guess at she had once transformed herself into an icon of glamour. Her cousin Delia hadn't achieved that elusive goal, had in fact made things worse, and Dixie, who welcomed strays and misfits with open arms, had welcomed her cousin.

"So, she needed a place to hide out and you, my sweet little softhearted Dixie, took her in," he said softly, trailing a forefinger down the slope of her nose.

Dixie scowled, not comfortable with the implied idea that she was a kind of saint. She was trying to be a decent sort of person, that was all, trying to right a few wrongs.

"Well, shoot," she said. "The poor homely little thing needed someone to look out for her. You ought to see her with her wig off. She looks like she just escaped from a prison camp."

Jake lovingly brushed the tangle of bangs back from her eyes, his heart warming. "She can't look any worse than that one-eyed cat of yours."

"No, I don't suppose she does," Dixie admitted with a chuckle.

He wrapped an arm around her shoulders and leaned down to kiss her lips and the tip of her nose. Dixie snuggled against him, burrowing her head into the hollow of his shoulder and wrapping her arms around him.

"It just about breaks my heart," she murmured sadly. "Dee knocks herself out to please Tyler. She ought to trust that man to love her no matter what. If he only loves her for her hair or her figure, then what kind of love is that? If that's the way he is, he isn't worth all the heartache. I wish she could see that. I wish . . ."

She let her wish trail off into nothingness and squeezed her eyes shut against a sudden wave of regret and misery. She wished so many things. She wished she'd never gone to Hollywood, that she'd never become so single-minded in her pursuit of fame that she had lost her perspective. She wished people had more sense than to think platinum-blond hair and a tiny waist could make them happy. She wished she could have made Dee see that before she'd turned herself bald. And she wished most of all that she could have made Jeanne see it before it had been too late.

"Hey." Jake tipped her chin up and stared down at the torment in her expression and felt something inside him tear in two. "It's not your fault, honey."

He wished he could tell her how much he meant it, but he couldn't tell her he knew she had been Devon Stafford. He couldn't tell her that the pieces of the mystery were finally starting to make sense, that he was beginning to have an idea of why she had left stardom behind. All he could do was hold her close and try to convince her by sheer strength of will.

Dixie mustered a smile for him, calling on talents she made little use of these days. "I didn't mean what I said about you being mean. You're about the sweetest man I know. Letting Eldon take care of your Porsche and letting Sylvie make such a fuss over you."

"I like Sylvie," he admitted. "I like all your friends."

She cocked an eyebrow. "Even Eldon?"

168

"Well . . . I'll reserve judgment on Eldon until I see what he does to my baby."

Dixie chuckled and hugged him. "You're a pretty decent fella for a California city boy. And so romantic, climbing up the side of my house like Zorro."

Jake made a face. "Next time I'm coming to the front door with flowers like any normal besotted man."

Dixie turned to face him, coming up on her knees on the mattress. She let the sheet fall away from her, her attention solely on Jake.

"Are you besotted? Really?" she asked, serious and so hopeful it scared her.

"You better believe it, lady," he said, stroking her short thick hair.

"I want to," Dixie whispered. "Oh, I surely do want to."

"Need some convincing, do you?"

Jake slid down, pulling her with him. He rolled her beneath him and distracted her by nuzzling her breasts while his hands swept the bedclothes, searching. He raised his head, grinning, a wicked gleam in his eyes, and dangled two little foil-wrapped packages over her nose. "Polka dots or paisley?"

Dixie lay awake, listening to the rain pelt the window and Jake's peaceful breathing.

She cuddled against him, her head pressed to his shoulder, one leg twined with his. Her arm had long since fallen asleep, but she couldn't bring herself to move away from him. He was so warm and solid. She wanted to cling to him as if he were a rock in a windstorm. Then again, the whirlwind swirling inside her was caused by him. How could he be both storm and shelter?

He was the last man she should have fallen for — demanding, perfectionistic, everything she had run away from. But he was also the only man she could have fallen for — sweet, strong, honest. She wanted to trust him with her life, with her secrets, but she was afraid to.

It was too soon. Everything had happened so fast. She hadn't even been thinking about romance. The quiet calming routine of her life here had lulled her into forgetting about things like magnetism and chemistry. Then Jake had burst in, sending all kinds of ripples across the calm waters of her existence. Her instincts told her to trust him, to let go, to love him, but her instincts had been wrong before.

Pictures of her days in Hollywood flashed across her memory like old vacation slides. Pictures of people she'd known, people she'd trusted, people who had turned out to have been looking out only for their own benefit. She remembered vividly her last conversation with her agent, a man she had trusted implicitly.

He had been in the process of negotiating a new contract for her with the producers of *Wylde Time*. They had been squawking about the twelve pounds she'd gained when she had quit smoking during the show's hiatus, saying it would look like twenty-five on film. They wanted the weight off before production began on the new season's shows, but she had balked at the idea, partly out of stubbornness, partly because she had begun to see that she had been virtually starving herself. Her health had begun to suffer from the unbalanced diet and the brutal workout schedule. She had been hospitalized briefly for exhaustion at the end of the previous season. A doctor had even warned her that dire things lay in her future if she went on as she had been doing. But the only thing the people around her had cared about was that she look like the same Devon Stafford who had already made them millions. It didn't matter to them that she felt better or that she thought the extra weight looked fine on her.

"I don't care what you have to do," her agent had said, his voice gravelly and low, his dark eyes burning with anger and the shadows of fear. "Starve yourself, take up smoking again for crying out loud. Lose the fat, babe, or we're out big bucks here. Do you understand me?"

She had understood all too well. In that moment she had looked at Al Altobelli and seen him for exactly what he was. He wasn't her friend. He wasn't her father. He was a man who had picked her stage name for her by closing his eyes and pointing to two dots on a map of England. He was a man who sold her to the highest bidder and pocketed ten percent. That was his business. *She* was just business, a name on a marquee, a face on a glossy poster.

Hell, it wasn't even her real face. It was a skeleton of her face, painted and polished, lips pumped full of saline and protein, eyes turned luminous green by the magic of optic science. Precious little Devon Stafford was the real Dee Ann Montrose, the girl who had grown up with the nickname Dixie back in the hills of North Carolina. The accent had been schooled out of her speech, her body had been honed down to the bone. The long platinum locks that men the world over dreamed about were mostly extensions, woven in and colored icy blond by a man named Eco.

All of it had come rushing home as she'd stood there watching Al rant, only half-listening as he'd thrust an article about an all-broccoli diet in her face and screamed at her to do something.

That was when the disillusionment had begun. It had come full circle in a cemetery as she'd stood alone watching strangers lower Jeanne Parmantel into a cold, black grave. No one else had bothered to come. No one else had cared, because who was Jeanne Parmantel, anyway? Just another little no-body who hadn't quite been good enough or thin enough or sexy enough. She hadn't been Devon Stafford. She hadn't been anybody.

The old pain tore through Dixie like a knife and she tightened her hold on Jake as tears squeezed past the barrier of her lashes. She clung to him as the storm buffeted her inside. She ached to tell him. She ached to have him hold her and rock her as she poured out her heart and her sorrow and all the guilt. But she was afraid. Deep down inside, in the innermost sacred room in her heart, she was afraid. She wanted so badly for him to love Dixie La Fontaine, she couldn't bring herself to tell him she had once been Devon Stafford.

Jake turned toward her, saying nothing, giving no indication that he was awake.

Without a word he hugged Dixie close and pressed a kiss in her hair. She hung on to him and cried, struggling to keep silent, to mask the ragged breathing and still the shaking of her shoulders. She was trying not to wake him, he knew. Whatever terrible pain was tormenting her was too personal to share.

It tore at him to hear her cry, to know she was suffering alone. His vibrant, perky Dixie with her bright eyes and sunny smile was crying in the night, hurting. Anger burned through him. He would have cheerfully strangled anyone who made Dixie cry. She was so sweet, so loyal, so good at heart, how could anyone be so callous as to hurt her?

Maybe no one had, he reflected, cooling his overheated protective instincts, calling on his brain to do a little of the work that had made his pseudonym famous. Perhaps the person who had hurt Dixie had been Devon Stafford. Maybe it was Devon Stafford she had run away from. Perhaps she simply had no longer been able to reconcile the image with the woman she really was.

But why would that make her cry as if she'd lost her last best friend in the world? If she had come here to make peace with herself, why was she lying in agony in his arms?

He wanted her to tell him. He wanted her to call to him now and confide in him here in the dark of her cluttered room with the rain driving against the house in sheets. He wanted to comfort her. He wanted to understand her. He wanted her to trust him enough to share her tears and the pain that wrung them from her. And it hurt him that she would share her body with him but not her soul.

He was falling in love. Real love. Sweet, tender love. This wasn't one of his mutual attractions that had led to a reasonable relationship with rules and bounds. There wasn't anything reasonable about the way he was feeling as he held Dixie and listened to her fight against her tears. This was love. He wanted her to give him everything she was, everything she had been. He wanted her to turn to him for protection and the shelter of his strength.

But she was crying in the night. Alone.

He couldn't take it. He really couldn't. He had been an officer in the Marines, trained to withstand enemy interrogation, toughened to resist torture, but the sound of Dixie's muffled, choked-back sobs was cutting him to ribbons. Pride be damned. He didn't care if she wouldn't tell him why. He just couldn't bear to let her go on any longer. He would rather have had the soles of his feet whipped than listen to Dixie try to smother the sound of her inner pain another second.

He brushed her hair back, wetting it with the tears he caught on his fingers, slicking the dark mass back from the delicate oval of her face. He pressed soft kisses to her eyelids, brushing his lower lip against the damp length of her lashes. He sipped the salty tears that trailed down the ripe curve of her cheek and met her swollen, trembling lips with a gentle kiss.

"Don't cry, baby," he murmured. "Don't cry."

"I'm sorry," Dixie whispered, aching with misery.

She hadn't wanted to disturb Jake's sleep and she certainly hadn't meant for him to catch her crying. She braced herself for his questions. Of course he would ask. She'd never known a man as inquisitive as Jake. He was always trying to see inside things, wondering what made people tick, asking little questions and looking for answers that went beyond the obvious. She'd chided him more than once for not looking beyond the surface, but she'd been wrong about him. She'd sat next to him at Sylvie's and watched and listened as he gathered bits of information about everyone there and ran them all through that logical brain of his, trying to put the pieces together. He'd done the same with her. Certainly now he would have more than enough reason to go looking for answers, answers she wasn't prepared to give.

But he didn't ask. He kissed her. And whispered to her, murmuring words of comfort. His hands stroked her body, soothing her, easing the tension from her muscles, warming the chill that shook her from within.

"Jake," she said. "Make love to me. Please."

She heard the note of desperation in her voice and thought that surely now he would ask her. She'd never felt more vulnerable and he had to have sensed that. But he didn't utter a word. He kissed her again, rolling over her with a slight shifting of his hips. He eased himself into her, giving her his heat, his strength.

They had come together before in a blaze of passion and they had come together in playfulness. This time was different still. Sweeter, gentler, as tender as a new green bud in spring.

Wanting only to comfort her, to transport her away from her pain, Jake was slow and careful, focusing his concentration on giving her pleasure. He stoked the fires gradually, his strokes smooth and measured.

Dixie lay beneath him, too spent to do anything but hold on. She fastened her hands on his waist, her fingers pressing into the taut, flexing muscles of the small of his back. She closed her eyes, letting sensation sweep away her doubts and her pain. She concentrated on the feel of him inside her, and when fulfillment came, the last of her anguish subsided.

Jake's body shuddered with his release and he relaxed against Dixie. She murmured his name and kissed his ear, but when he turned his head to kiss her she was already asleep.

His mind stirring with questions and feelings, he turned with her in his arms and settled in for the last hours of the night, still joined with her body, still longing to touch her soul.

Nine

Dixie beamed up at their waitress, Miss Divine Trulove. Miss Divine smiled back at her like a grandmother, small blue eyes twinkling. The sun streaming in the window across the room turned her puff of white hair into a halo around her head. She looked as if she had just stepped out of a Norman Rockwell painting.

"Good mornin', Dixie love," Miss Divine said loudly. She plucked her order pad and stubby pencil out of the pocket of her ruffled muslin apron and lifted them up under her slim nose.

"Good mornin', Miss Divine," Dixie answered, matching the volume of the elderly lady's voice. "I'll have a great big piece of chocolate pecan pie with lots of whipped cream and a big glass of milk."

"For breakfast?" Jake sat across the table from her, looking shocked and disgusted.

Miss Divine snatched his menu away and smacked him on the shoulder with it. "Our Dixie may have whatever she likes for breakfast, Mr. Gannon," she declared, scowling at him ferociously.

"Yes, ma'am," he mumbled, ducking his head in chagrin.

"We don't cotton much to strangers coming down here telling us what to do," she said primly. Her voice was smooth with the polish of a true Southern lady, but a blade of steel ran through it as strong as any general's sword. She straightened the small silk bow at the throat of her dainty flowered dress, her stern eye still on Jake, waiting for a response.

"No, ma'am," he said.

Miss Divine sniffed and sighed in apparent satisfaction with his reply. She turned the page of her green order pad, wetting the tip of her pencil with the very end of her tongue and poising it exactly four inches from her face. "Now, Mr. Gannon, what would you like for breakfast this fine mornin'?"

"Orange juice, whole wheat toast and a bowl of cornflakes with strawberries, please."

"Peach slices," she corrected him. "The strawberries are a might soft today. Besides all those little strawberry seeds aren't good for your gallbladder."

Jake blinked at her.

She wrote the order with painstaking care, as if someone were going to judge her penmanship. As she tucked the pad in the pocket of her apron she gave Jake a nod. "And I'll bring you some eggs and bacon and hashed browns. A man needs to keep up his strength. And some grits too. They're good for your constitution. And you will eat it all or else I will know the reason why."

Dixie giggled at the look on Jake's face as their feisty, eighty-five-year-old hostess made her way back toward the kitchen, her orthopedic shoes scuffing against the old yellow linoleum.

"Miss Divine was once the dean of a school for incorrigible boys. She'll take a switch to you if you don't mind your manners."

Jake scowled at her. "She wants me to eat like a lumberjack and she lets you order pie for breakfast. Chocolate pecan pie for breakfast! Do you have any idea of the amount of fat and sugar in something like that?"

Her brows drew together like storm clouds. "No, and if you tell me I'll get my gun out and pistol-whip you. Just because you're a health terrorist doesn't give you the right to spoil my fun."

"I only mentioned it because I care about you," Jake said. "That stuff is not good for you, honey."

"Well, I don't order it every day," Dixie

protested, her anger dissipating at his confession. He cared about her. He didn't want her ruining her health. That was sweet even if she did resent his disapproval of her eating habits. She gave him a coy look from under her lashes, tilting her head and smiling at him. Under the table she rubbed his calf with the toes of one stockinged foot. "Today is special. I'm celebrating . . . us."

He reached for her hand and smiled back at her. Her charm was irresistible, as powerful as anything he'd ever come up against. It was every bit as strong in person as it was on the screen, even without benefit of the glamorous Stafford image. She made him feel overwhelmingly masculine and protective and possessive and hot as hell. He leaned across the table, his gaze on her mouth.

"What about us are you celebrating?" he asked, his voice low and husky, his eyes glittering with teasing lights.

Dixie shivered visibly and leaned toward him, arching her neck and nibbling her lip. "You know what," she murmured breathlessly.

"Do I? Maybe you should show me."

"Jake. This is a public place," she whispered, pretending to be scandalized by his behavior while thrills raced up and down her spine.

Jake gave a wicked chuckle low in his throat and leaned closer. "Is it? I can only see you, sweetheart."

Suddenly Eldon's meaty red face popped over the back of the booth. Dixie gave a little squeak of surprise, her hand coming up to keep her heart from leaping out of her chest. Jake slouched back in his seat and glared at the mechanic.

"Excuse me, Dixie, can I borrow your ketchup?" he asked, eyeing Jake as if he were a junkyard dog.

Dixie handed him the ketchup bottle over her shoulder.

"This fella givin' you a hard time, honey?"

"No, Eldon."

"He givin' you something else he hadn't oughta be?"

Dixie turned, her cheeks as red as the contents of the bottle Elton held in his grimy hand. "Thank you for your concern, Eldon," she said stiffly. "But would you kindly mind your own business?"

Elton gave Jake a long meaningful I-still-have-your-Porsche-at-my-mercy look, then slid back down on his side of the booth. Dixie rolled her eyes. Jake growled a little under his breath.

"I'm sorry," she said with a sheepish look. "He's just —"

"Looking out for you, is all," Jake finished. He reached over and tweaked her cheek to let her know he wasn't angry, then settled in his seat to think.

How many of the good folks of Mare's Nest knew Dixie's other identity? he wondered. How many of them had she trusted with her secret? It warmed his heart to think of how they had taken her in and treated her like a beloved daughter, cossetting and protecting her, indulging her and looking out for her well-being. But it made him feel like an outsider as well, not just in Mare's Nest, but in Dixie's life. When would she trust him enough to tell him her secret? How long would it take before he became a part of her family?

Guilt nipped at him as he glanced around the little cafe. He took in the dark green and pink ruffled chintz curtains at the windows, the neat little tables with their menu holders and condiments arranged just so. Most of the patrons sat near the counter, sipping their morning coffee and chatting in their pleasant lazy drawls. Miss Cora May Trulove perched on a stool at the counter, fiddling with the volume knob on a portable color television. Miss Divine slapped at her hand as the daytime version of *Wheel of Fortune* came on.

Dixie's friends were looking out for her,

trying to protect her. And who was he? The wolf in sheep's clothing, sneaking in among them to snatch their little lamb. A writer looking for a story. But the book was no longer his primary objective, he admitted as he stared at Dixie, whose attention had been snagged by a loose thread on the cuff of her blouse. He wanted to know all her mysteries because he was obsessed with her, because he had to know everything about her or feel incomplete . . . because he loved her.

"What?" she said, looking up at him, her brows drawing together. "Have I got something on my face?" she asked, rubbing her chin with her fist. "I knew I shouldn't have monkeyed with that kitchen faucet before we left. I've got grease on me again, haven't I?"

"You look fine," Jake murmured, resting his forearms on the tabletop. "I think you're absolutely beautiful."

She actually blushed. He couldn't believe it. She had to have been told that same line by some of the most famous men in the world and yet she was blushing. Of course, she had been Devon Stafford then, the sex symbol, the actress. And now she was just Dixie La Fontaine, innocent and uncertain.

"I love you," he said softly, simply, honestly, never taking his eyes from hers.

He hadn't planned on telling her. The feeling was still too new to him. But the words had just come out, had been drawn out by the look in her eyes.

Dixie felt all the blood drain right out of her head. Her mouth fell open and her eyes grew round. She stared at Jake. He sat there in a casual pose, but there was a tension in the set of his broad shoulders and in the line of his strong jaw. The intensity of his eyes was enough to take a woman's breath away. And, oh my, he was handsome. His golden hair had been tossed a little by the morning breeze and he hadn't bothered to comb it with more than his fingers. He wore a white T-shirt with a faded blue chambray shirt over it, the cuffs rolled back three times to reveal strong tanned forearms. A gold watch was strapped to his wrist; the hair on his arm curled around the face of it like delicate scrollwork.

He loved her.

Dixie blinked as her vision swam a bit. Wasn't it just like him to make a statement like that, calm as you please, and then sit there watching her, looking right inside her with those laser-blue eyes of his.

He loved her.

"Oh, my," she whispered.

His expression softened as he looked at her. Dimples creased his cheeks and he chuckled to himself. "I guess you weren't expecting that."

Expecting it? She had let herself dream about it a little, but no, she hadn't let herself expect it. She had given up having expectations. They were dangerous. There was too much potential for disappointment and it hurt too badly when that disappointment came. No, she hadn't expected to hear him say it, but it filled her with a golden warmth just the same.

"That doesn't mean I didn't want to hear it," she whispered.

"Good," he said in that decisive way of his that made Dixie wonder if he'd ever been uncertain of anything in his life. He seemed so strong, so . . . perfect.

Fear grabbed her by the throat like a fist. After so many months of quiet solitude she suddenly felt as if her life were bolting off like a runaway horse, dragging her along with it. And complications thundered in a big herd right behind her, just waiting to trample her in the stampede.

Love could be a wonderful thing and it could be disastrous. It could be exhilarating or terrifying. Fear surged through Dixie like ice water in her veins. Her whole way of life hung in the balance because she had fallen in love with a handsome stranger. What did she know about Jake Gannon other than what he made her feel? Love meant sharing everything, trusting another person with your most delicate feelings and deepest secrets, sharing flaws and dreams and pasts, baring the most tender parts of heart and soul and trusting the other person not to hurt you. With Jake it meant trusting a man she barely knew.

I didn't come here to hurt you, Dixie. The line came back to her as clearly as if he'd only just said it.

The customers at the counter were shouting encouragement to a contestant on *Wheel of Fortune.* Miss Cora May announced the answer to the puzzle and gave a rebel yell, as if she'd won herself a new Mercedes. Miss Divine came toward them, half bent over, her slender back bowed like a willow branch by the weight of the tray with their breakfast on it.

"Can I get a refill on my coffee when you have a minute, Miss Divine?" Eldon shouted as she passed.

"No. All that acid is bad for your stomach, Eldon Baines."

"Yes, ma'am."

Jake got to his feet to take the tray. "I'll

take that for you, Miss Divine," he shouted. "We don't want you to miss your program."

She gave him a look of approval, then slanted Dixie a smile and a wink. "I believe you may have a good one here, Dixie love. Even if he is from California."

Dixie dug up a smile for her friend. "I hope so, Miss Divine. I hope so."

They fell into a routine over the next week. Jake would run on the beach with the dogs in the morning, then Dixie would walk with him as he cooled down. They would share a cup of coffee and talk with Sylvie and sometimes Fabiano, if he wasn't busy with his t'ai chi or his art. Then Dixie would go off to fix somebody's washing machine or run on a call for Eldon or just go visiting her friends, leaving Jake to work on his mystery novel. In the evening they would walk on the beach again, returning to his cottage to make love.

It was a comfortable arrangement, Jake had to admit, but there were a few details that left him feeling unsettled. Eldon hadn't finished with his Porsche, Dixie hadn't told him she loved him, and the name Devon Stafford had not been raised.

He counseled himself to give her time. He had no deadlines in his life. He told himself he couldn't expect her to simply let go of a secret she had kept from the rest of the world for over a year. And yet it gnawed at him. Her lack of trust hurt him and at the same time it kept him from telling her about his own other identity. If she didn't trust him enough to tell him, she didn't trust him enough to hear his confession either.

Somewhere along the line he had given up the idea of writing the Devon Stafford story. The more he knew Dixie, the deeper he fell in love with her, the less he wanted to share her with other people. He had thought the world might benefit from getting to know the woman behind the glamorous Devon Stafford image, and no doubt they would, but still he wanted her all to himself.

It seemed a completely miraculous thing to him, falling in love. He had never given it very much thought until now, until he'd fallen like a rock for a curvy minx who turned her nose up at all his sensible habits. He had always assumed he would end up with a woman who shared his views on fitness and health and orderliness and logic. But Dixie detested the idea of strenuous exercise, she ate whatever she had a craving for, and the concept of neatness escaped her entirely. She was his opposite in almost every way and he was crazy about her.

He dug around now in the box that held all his notes and files, the box he had largely ignored since his arrival in Mare's Nest. He shuffled through the photographs and news clippings, comparing the Hollywood star to the woman he knew. He had a difficult time picturing Dixie as being happy in Hollywood. Compared to what she had here, the life of a star would seem foreign and phony. It pained him to think of Dixie living among the sharks. The entertainment business was tough and competitive, every man for himself. He knew she had been hurt by it, and the very idea was like a knife in his heart.

He singled out the most recent picture of Devon Stafford, a shot taken by a tabloid photographer as she'd come out of a meeting with her agent. She'd looked right at the camera, the famous green eyes brimming with tears and defiance and a pain that cut him to the quick, the pouting lips turning downward. He thought she looked too thin to be healthy even though she'd already gained weight after quitting smoking. She looked miserable and he wished she were in the room with him right that minute so he could have gathered her close and offered her comfort.

The screen door banged behind him and he dropped the photograph into the box, closed the top of the carton and lifted it onto a shelf above his desk.

"I promise I won't peek," Dixie said. She came up behind him, wound her arms around his waist and rubbed her cheek against his back, inhaling deeply of the warm, masculine scent of him.

"I'll let you read it when I'm done," he said, turning and looping his arms around her. "Before anybody else gets to see it. How's that?"

Excitement lit her face. "Will you? I'd like that. I'd —"

Dixie broke off at the look on Jake's face. He looked strained, upset, as if he were laboring under a terrible emotion. She reached up and rubbed the worry line etched between his brows. She stroked his cheek. "Sugar, what's wrong?"

He sighed and shook his head, mustering a weary smile. "Nothing. I was just kind of wrapped up thinking about my heroine."

"Oh. What's she like?"

He thought about that for a minute, his eyes taking on that searching quality. "She's . . . a little lost, uncertain. She's still kind of a mystery to me. Something is haunting her, but I haven't figured out what."

Dixie frowned. She wanted to say she knew someone like that, that she was someone like that, but she held her tongue. Instead she scratched the tip of her nose and gave him a curious look. "You're making her up out of your head and you don't know?"

"Sometimes it works that way."

"I'll bet that just drives you crazy," she said, teasing.

He smiled at her, a soft, gentle smile, and brushed her bangs out of her eyes. "Yeah, but I'll work it out. What are you up to?"

"Nothing special. I thought maybe if you weren't in the throes of some creative fit you might want to go for a boat ride. I thought we could take my old power boat over to Horse Island and have us a picnic supper."

"I like that idea very much. I'll provide the supper."

Dixie scowled at him. "It won't be made out of tofu or some awful stuff like that, will it? Because I'll warn you right now, I won't eat it. And if you come near me with a stalk of broccoli I won't be held responsible for my actions."

"Don't get a bee in your bonnet. You can bring the dessert, so if I bring anything too healthy you can still get your quota of processed sugar. How's that sound?"

"Sounds like you're making fun of me, that's how it sounds," she said, pouting.

"That's not it at all. I want to contribute to

the outing. I can't run a boat so it has to be something else. Now, if you still think I'm making fun of your sweet tooth you can feel free to take a poke at my dubious mechanical abilities." He hooked a finger under her chin and tilted her face up. "Okay?"

"I'm sorry," she said sheepishly. "It's just that sometimes I think about how you're such a fitness fanatic and that maybe you wished I'd go running and live on celery and hone myself down to some ridiculous anorexic shape."

"Then you wouldn't be my Dixie, would you?" he said, leaning down to kiss her, running his hands lovingly down her back and over the flare of her hips. He growled appreciatively, nibbling her throat, his fingers cupping and kneading her buttocks. "I happen to love your shape, lady. Can't you tell?"

Dixie groaned as he pulled her hips against his and let her feel his growing arousal. She met his kiss hungrily, opening her mouth for him and welcoming the thrust of his tongue. Time spun away as they concentrated on pleasing each other. Jake finally lifted his head a fraction to draw a breath. Dixie smiled against his lips and hugged him, blinking back the sudden threat of tears. "Sometimes I think you're just too good to be true, Jake Gannon."

He gave her a roguish smile. "Yeah. It's my one great flaw."

They agreed to meet behind the beach house at two o'clock. Jake borrowed the Bronco to run into town in order to procure their supper. Meanwhile, Dixie packed the picnic basket with utensils and a container of homemade caramels, fudge, and pralines. Sylvie supervised, sitting at the kitchen table nibbling on a piece of fudge and clucking like a fussy old mother hen.

"I tell you, Dixie, I only want what's best for you. You know this. You're like my own daughter to me, only you haven't ripped my heart out by marrying into a family of gangsters like my Riva."

"I thought she married a stockbroker."

"There's a difference?" Sylvie sniffed and shrugged, flipping one bejeweled hand. "I would never give you bad advice, Dixie. God forbid I should ever give you bad advice. You have to tell him."

"I know I do," Dixie said reluctantly. She picked up a dish towel and mopped up the water that had leaked out of the faucet handle. She was going to have to replace the cartridge, that was all there was to that, she thought absently. "I'm just not ready, is all."

"What are you waiting for, the apocalypse?"

She rubbed the countertop with her towel, trying to concentrate on the motion instead of the rising tide of fear inside her. "It's hard, Sylvie. I like having him love me, Dixie, just the way I am. I'm afraid if I tell him about Devon Stafford, then he'll want me to be her and I can't do that again. I won't. Not for anything."

"What makes you think he'd want Devon instead of Dixie?"

Dixie gave a humorless laugh. "Devon Stafford is Jake's idea of the ideal woman. I know he says he likes me fine, but if he had the chance to have Devon Stafford don't you think he'd grab it?"

"He loves you, sweetheart," Sylvie said softly, coming to stand behind her. She put her hands on Dixie's shoulders and gave her an affectionate squeeze. "You can't keep secrets from him. My Sid, God rest his soul, always said more harm is done in this world by secrets than anything else. Tell him. Today."

"Maybe, I will," she said, only to placate Sylvie. She checked her watch and gave a little gasp. "Oh, my, look at the time. Jake'll be here any minute."

She scooped up the picnic basket and her bomber jacket and strode purposefully out of the kitchen, weaving her way through the array of collections in the dining room and living room. Cyclops ran after her, making broken oboe noises. Sylvie followed, still nibbling on her fudge. Dixie swung the porch door open, letting out the cat, then yanked it back shut as a black pickup roared into her yard.

"Oh, my Lord! It's Tyler Holt!"

"Is Delia here?" Sylvie asked.

"No. She's gone down to Charleston to see about getting hair implants."

Sylvie muttered something under her breath in Yiddish. "These people. See what a mess they make with all these secrets?"

Dixie scowled at her and forced herself to take a step outside. She couldn't decide which was worse: facing Tyler Holt or accepting the reality of Sylvie's words. She chose the former. At least she could buffalo Tyler with her acting abilities.

As she started down the steps Jake drove in, parked beside the pickup and got out of the Bronco, eyeing Holt with his jealous-male look. Tyler ignored him and stalked toward Dixie, his eyes narrowed, mouth curving down. Tall with dark wavy hair and dark eyes, he was a handsome man when he wasn't looking petulant.

"Where is she?" he demanded.

Dixie struck a belligerent pose, dangling

the picnic basket from her fingertips and tilting her head back. "Who?"

"Who?" He snorted. "You know damn well who! Delia."

"She's not here." She gave him a cool look. "I told you that before, Tyler."

"Yeah, well . . ."

He trailed off, his eyes darting as if he might see the words he needed for his argument scrawled somewhere. Dixie sighed. Tyler Holt was not exactly a brilliant conversationalist on his best day. From what she knew of him, he didn't have the brain God gave a goat. Aside from his looks, she couldn't imagine what Dee wanted with him, but there was no accounting for taste. Dixie put more stock in the inner person, but she'd learned her lessons about that the hard way.

"Has she called you?" she asked.

"Yeah, but she won't tell me where she is and it's driving me crazy."

Dixie gave a lazy shrug and combed her hair back with one hand. "If she won't tell you, then I've got to figure she don't want you to know."

He glared at her and wagged a threatening finger in her face. "If she's calling from here, I can find out, you know. I got me a buddy works for the phone company and he can trace any call he wants to just like that."

198

Dixie sniffed. "Oh, you're so full of hot air, Tyler Holt, I don't know why you don't just float away."

He sighed and made a face as he looked down at Cyclops, seemingly considering his options. Intimidation had failed. Anger had failed. His shoulders drooped as the aggression drained out of him in another long sigh. When he turned back to Dixie the look in his eyes just about broke her heart.

"Come on, Dixie, tell me, please. I miss her something awful. She won't tell me why she ran off. I can't sleep nights for thinking it was something I did."

Dixie nibbled at her lip. She could see Jake casually leaning against the hood of the Bronco, watching her intently. She swallowed hard.

"I'm sorry, Tyler," she said, softly, letting the act slide. "I can't tell you. It's between you and Dee. You'll just have to work it out with her."

Tyler stared glumly at his boots, hands on his hips. He worked his jaw and sighed again, then turned and went back to his truck, sparing Jake a belligerent glance.

Dixie watched him go, all the secrets she was forced to keep weighing down in her stomach like a brick. Bob Dog pushed a wet nose into her hand, looking up at her with sympathetic eyes. She stroked his dark head, then bent to shoo Cyclops out of the picnic basket.

"Why didn't you tell him?" Jake asked, taking the basket from her and stowing it in the back seat with the cooler.

"I couldn't. I promised Dee."

Jake turned with his hand on the open door of the truck. "The man is in pain, Dixie. He loves her. Don't you think he deserves to know the truth?"

"It's not my place to tell him."

"What about all your talk about trust? You're the one who said she should trust him to love her no matter what."

"I can't make that decision for her."

"Only for yourself," he muttered.

"What does that mean?"

He looked away and shook his head. "Nothing. I just think you could have taken a little pity on the poor guy."

Dixie scowled at him. "Oh, you men. Y'all stick together like flies in a glue pot, don't you? It was Tyler started this mess in the first place."

She stomped around the hood of the Bronco and hauled herself up into the driver's seat, adjusting it with a yank. Jake climbed in on the other side and slammed the door.

"It's his fault Delia's hair fell off?" he said sarcastically.

"It's his fault she tried to look like something she wasn't," Dixie snapped. *And mine,* she added silently, miserably. She let her head fall back against the seat and sighed, all the fight draining out of her. Keeping her own secret from Jake was bad enough; she didn't want to argue with him about other people's problems as well.

"Can we not fight about this?" she asked. "I wanted today to be fun. I just wanted us to have a nice afternoon."

Jake sighed and rubbed the back of his neck. "I'm sorry. I didn't meant to start a fight. It's none of my business anyway. I just don't like people keeping secrets from each other," he said softly.

Dixie stared out the windshield. She could see Sylvie standing on the porch watching them. She could see a wedge of beach, sea, and sky, Abby and Hobbit nosing around the stilts the house sat on, Bob Dog lying on his back with his paws curled against him. She thought about her life here with her menagerie of misfits.

She could have told Jake now, could have just blurted it out. *You think Delia and Tyler have secrets, how about this — I used to be Devon Stafford.* But she was too uncertain about what would happen after she'd dropped the bomb. She was too afraid of what the fallout would be and she wanted too much to have this afternoon with him. She wanted Dixie La Fontaine to have him to herself for just a little while longer. So she kept her silence and turned the ignition key.

Ten

"Why is it called Horse Island?"

Dixie looked around, snagging her wind-tossed hair back with one hand. It was a small island that didn't boast much of anything besides sand, scrub grass, and a thick growth of trees, but it had its own small natural bay and a dock — and it was all hers.

"Back in the days when the Spanish were cruising around here with galleons, one used to sink every once in a while," she said as they reached the dock. "These waters are full of old wrecks. One went down off this island in 1567. All hands were lost, but some of the horses they'd been transporting managed to swim ashore. They lived here for years on their own, wild as cobs, so folks just got to calling it Horse Island. Then a man named John Bascomb got it into his head he could round them up, break them and sell them. 'Course the only thing he broke was his own fool neck. They say his ghost still wanders around here, but I've never seen him. He probably knows I think he was an idiot."

"No doubt," Jake agreed with an indulgent smile.

Dixie watched him heft the cooler up onto the dock, biceps bulging against the sleeves of his purple cotton shirt. The ride over had been pleasant enough, the tension between them dissipating as the bow of the boat had lifted and cut through the slate blue water.

She felt as if she'd been given a reprieve from death row. She didn't like arguing with Jake and she didn't like keeping secrets from him. She didn't like the idea of revealing those secrets either, so she was caught in a trap of her own making. But she had her own agenda concerning getting herself out of that snare. It was part of the reason she had brought him to the island — to start easing herself out of her predicament a little bit at a time in a place where she had always felt a certain peace.

Jake hauled himself up on the dock, then gave Dixie a hand up. She tied off the boat, then they gathered their gear and started toward the beach. Dixie kept her eyes on the boards, picking out the ones she had replaced with her own two hands and smiling at them as if they were her children. She had spent a good deal of her time on the island thinking, hurting, healing. Working on the dock had been the first step she'd taken toward rebuilding her life. She had wanted to do something that was literally constructive, to work with her hands and see the result.

"This is a special place for you, isn't it?" Jake said as he sat the cooler down on the sand near the charred remains of an old campfire.

Dixie's step faltered a bit. She put the picnic basket and woolen blanket down, wondering just how much he really saw with that intense gaze of his.

"Yes," was all she said. She snapped the red plaid blanket open and kneeled with it as it fluttered to the ground.

"I can see why. It's very peaceful."

It was that, Dixie thought as she rummaged through the picnic basket, digging out the goodies. She selected a praline and nibbled on the sugary treat as she looked around. The wind was coming strong out of the southeast, blowing up a storm. The ride over had been choppy, and her old boat had bucked against the small whitecaps. But this spot was sheltered by a tangle of forest. It was a haven that had always given her a sense of calm. She clung to that as if it were a security blanket.

Jake knelt beside her and wrapped an arm around her shoulders, urging her to lay her head on his shoulder. "Thanks for bringing me to your special place."

She smiled up at him and raised the last bite of her treat to his lips. "Have a praline."

He let her feed it to him, licking the tips of her fingers, his gaze holding hers. "Mmmm . . . sweet," he murmured. "But not as sweet as you."

He bent his head and kissed her, both of them tasting of brown sugar and pecans. Dixie licked her lips when he raised his head.

"You're pretty sweet yourself, sugar," she said, cuddling against him.

They gathered wood for a fire, walking side by side in companionable silence. Dixie could feel him watching her, waiting, searching. Perhaps he sensed she had brought him here for a reason, but he didn't ask, he just waited.

What a far cry he was from the men she had known back in her Devon Stafford days. His penetrating gaze was at once reassuring and unnerving. It pleased her that he cared enough to look, but she was frightened of what he might see.

With other men she had always been able to hide, if not behind her looks, then certainly behind her talent as an actress. She wasn't sure she would be able to hide from

Jake for long. If they were to build anything lasting, she knew she couldn't. But she kept getting the feeling she was going to take that first step and fall into an abyss, so she kept pulling herself back from the edge. The words kept rising up in her throat, clogging there like a logjam, only to be swallowed back. She delayed the inevitable on the excuse of enjoying her afternoon with Jake, but she enjoyed the time only half as much because of the nervous anticipation churning inside her.

Jake had the fire going in no time. It crackled and popped pleasantly as the ocean hissed against the shore, and warmed them as they settled side by side on the blanket.

"My compliments, Mr. Gannon. You start a wonderful fire," Dixie said, cuddling against him.

"Gee, and I haven't even taken off your clothes yet," Jake quipped, bending down to nip her neck.

Giggling, Dixie socked him on the arm. "That's not what I meant."

"Ouch!" he complained. "You're getting as bad as Sylvie."

"Well, you deserved it. I compliment you on your talent with a few sticks of wood and some matches and you turn it into innuendo."

"It's a skill I picked up in the Marine Corps."

"Innuendo? Oh, that'll come in handy during a time of war," she said. "You can cut the enemy to ribbons with your rapier wit."

Jake grabbed her and tickled her ribs, his fingers sneaking inside her jacket. "This is what you get for being insubordinate."

Dixie gasped and squirmed. "They taught you this too? My, they're letting some funny boys in the Corps these days. What ever became of those 'few good men'? Couldn't they find any?"

"Hey." Nose to nose with her, he gave her his most ferocious mock scowl. "No defaming the Corps or I won't feed you."

"No need to get nasty," Dixie said, sitting back and straightening her jacket with a tug at the waistband.

Jake picked up a pebble and flung it toward the surf. "My old man would put you on bread and water for a week."

"He was a Marine too?"

"Was, is, always will be from now until the end of time, amen. Brigadier General Thaddeus J. Gannon."

"What made you leave?" She pushed a strand of hair back from his eyes and studied him. "With your love for order and fitness and all, you certainly seem like a career man."

He sighed and stared out at the ocean. The look in his eyes seemed wistful, rueful. "Yeah, that's what Dad always thought, too."

"How did he take it when you left?"

He gave a little bark of laughter. "I'll let you know the next time he decides to speak to me. We currently hold our conversations through my mother. 'Tell your son he's pig-headed,'" he snapped in a gruff imitation of his father. "'Tell Dad I know who I got it from.'"

He sighed, his big shoulders rising and falling. "A career in the Corps was what I had planned. Sometimes plans just don't live up to your expectations. I woke up one day and found myself wanting something that wasn't there. I had to go find it. Even if it meant giving up a lot, I had to do it or spend my whole life feeling as if something was missing." He turned toward her, those calm blue eyes intent and watchful. "Do you know what I mean?"

"Yeah," Dixie said quietly, dodging his gaze. She poked at the fire with a stick of driftwood, sending a shower of orange sparks into the air. "I know what you mean. You're lucky you found it."

Jake watched as her mind drifted away to a distant place that cast a sad shadow over her eyes and tugged at the corners of her mouth. He could have probed now. His interviewing instincts told him he would get answers, that the window of opportunity was open, but he didn't ask the questions. He waited. He wanted the story to come from Dixie willingly. The minutes passed excruciatingly, but he waited anyway. The truth had to come from her, not be dragged from her.

She dropped her stick and hooked a finger through the fine gold chain she wore. She lifted out the sea star and rubbed it between her thumb and forefinger in a gesture he'd seen her use many times.

"The friend that gave this to me," she began, still staring at the fire. "Her name was Jeanne Parmantel. We got to be friends when we were working together as waitresses out in L.A. She was from a little hill town in Georgia. She wanted to be an actress. She'd been the star of everything back home. Folks had thrown her a party to send her off to Hollywood. They were all sure she'd be a big star. But she never did make it.

"Every day she woke up wanting something acting could give her that nothing else could. Every night when she came home she was still just a waitress. It didn't matter what she did, what she tried, what lengths she was willing to go to. She was just never quite right for the part."

She sniffed and gave him a tremulous smile. "See how lucky you are, finding what you wanted. I mean, I know you haven't sold that mystery yet, but you're a writer and that's what you wanted."

"What happened to your friend?" Jake asked quietly, gently. If she refused to tell him it would be like a hammer blow to his heart.

She looked at the fire again as if she could see the memories there in the flames. "She took it hard. She'd been the prettiest girl back in Georgia, but there are lots of pretty girls in Hollywood. She was just another face. But she was determined. She did everything she could think of. She took classes, she starved herself, she worked out, she dyed her hair, she had plastic surgery. She used to joke she had enough plastic in her to qualify her as a walking Tupperware party. She wanted it so bad and she was so proud. . . ."

Tears spilled over the dam of her lashes and a knot of pain lodged in her throat as memories assailed her. Jeanne, so stubborn, determined to make it, but not willing to take favors from her friend who *had* made it.

She squeezed the sea star until the spines

of the individual arms dug into her fingers. "She gave me this for Christmas our first year out there and she said, 'See this, Dixie. This is what I'm gonna be — a star.' But all she ever was was a waitress."

She stopped and fought back another wave of misery. It beat against her relentlessly, battering the defense she had built against it. "She killed herself," she whispered. "December 22, 1989."

Hugging her knees, she put her head down then and cried for the friend she'd lost and for herself. A day didn't go by that she didn't blame herself. Hadn't Jeanne just followed her example? They had both driven themselves to terrible lengths to achieve what other people thought of as perfection. What Jeanne had lost sight of was that she'd been perfectly wonderful to start with. She'd thought she had to be another Devon Stafford. But the world didn't need another Devon Stafford, it needed one Jeanne Parmantel, and now she was lost forever.

If only . . . if only . . . The words played in Dixie's head like a record with the needle stuck in the groove. If only she had realized sooner what was really important. If only she had been able to convince Jeanne. If only she had been there when Jeanne had needed her in that darkest hour when death had seemed preferable to the pain of failure. *If only . . .*

She felt Jake's arm slide around her shoulders, but he didn't try to pull her up. He just held her, stroking her hair in a slow, soothing motion. He didn't try to tell her it was all right. He let her have her moment of privacy. He let her grieve and Dixie loved him for it. She had shared with him the most painful thing in her past, but he hadn't trespassed on it. No matter how much it hurt, it was *her* memory of Jeanne, something she needed to hold on to intact. She didn't want anyone trying to dismantle it with platitudes; she wanted understanding.

When the moment had passed, when she had endured the worst of the pain, she turned to him. She went into his arms and pressed her cheek against his chest. Now she needed his comfort and he gave it without reserve, wrapping her up in his warmth and solid strength.

"I miss her so much," she whispered, setting off another torrent of tears.

"I know, baby," Jake murmured into her hair.

He held her and rocked her, staring into the fire. It tore him up to hear her cry, to know that she blamed herself for her friend's death. All along he had suspected something was haunting her, but he had never guessed it would be anything so terrible, so wrenching as this guilt. He could feel it twist inside him as surely as if it had been his own. He would have done anything to take it away from her, but there was no way to do it. She clung to it and punished herself with it, at the same time trying to make amends by taking in misfits and outcasts and imperfect creatures. He had nothing to heal her with but time and love.

He tilted her face up and kissed her tears away. He gave her his handkerchief. She blew her nose, wadded up the previously immaculate white linen in her fist, and let her head fall against Jake's shoulder as her breathing calmed down. He brushed her hair and kissed her temple.

"We can't live other people's lives for them," he said, thinking not only of Dixie and her friend, but of himself and his father.

"No. But sometimes it would make life a whole lot easier."

"It seems to me we've got our hands full just trying to run our own lives." He ran his hands up her rib cage and filled them with her breasts. Gently kneading the plump globes, he gave her a playful little smile and waggled his brows. "I've certainly got my hands full."

Dixie smiled as his teasing coaxed a giggle from her. He really was a good man, a good friend. He had allowed her her grief and now he was tugging her gently away from it, wooing her back from the past and into the present. Jeanne was a memory never to be forgotten, but reality was Jake, with her here and now.

A low sound of pleasure hummed in her throat as his fingers massaged her breasts, his thumbs rubbing across the tips. She leaned toward him as he lowered his mouth to hers. It was the softest of kisses, warm and tender and sweet. It drew up her hunger for life and chased away the darkness of her memories. It offered her understanding and comfort and invited her to celebrate life rather than mourn death.

She wound her arms around Jake's neck and pulled herself up onto her knees. He turned onto his knees as well, never breaking the kiss or the caress. She met his tongue in a play that drifted back and forth from being lazy to eager. She ate up the taste of him, thinking she could never get enough if she lived to be a hundred.

His fingers left her breasts, moving to the buttons on her flannel shirt. He popped them free and tugged the tails from her jeans. His hands were cold and Dixie shivered as he touched her, stroking her sides and her tummy. Shivers raced through her, pooling in the pit of her stomach.

He struggled for a second with the front catch of her bra, then it gave way and she gasped into his mouth as her breasts spilled into the cool air and his cool hands. Despite the chill of his touch, the feel of his long fingers squeezing and petting stoked the fire in her blood until she was panting.

She tugged impatiently at his shirt, needing to touch him, to feel her skin against his, to press her body to his. But he held her at bay when she would have moved up against his bared chest. She ran her hands over him eagerly, loving the feel of taut flesh and rippling muscles. She traced her fingertips over his pectorals and drew her thumbs across his flat male nipples, delighting in the way the flesh pebbled beneath her touch. She tried once again to bring herself up against him, but he held her back, his hands still cupping her breasts.

Dixie pulled her mouth from his and trailed kisses down his chest. She drew her fingertips along his waistband, smiling at the way he sucked in a breath each time she dipped inside his jeans. His belly tightened as she traced circles around his navel and toyed with the metal button just below.

Bending down, she pressed her open mouth to his stomach and popped the button of his jeans. She worked the zipper down, easing over the straining bulge there. She followed suit with his briefs, slipping them down, teasing him, stroking him until his whole body was shuddering. Chuckling wickedly against his belly, she closed one small hand over him, caressing him with the gentlest of touches.

Jake drew in a sharp breath, his nostrils filling with the salty musky scent of the sea and arousal. He squeezed his eyes shut and tangled his fingers in Dixie's hair and massaged the back of her head, concentrating on the pleasure. Her breath was warm and moist against his groin, her lips like wet silk. He groaned and shuddered again, his whole body trembling as if the ground beneath him were moving in a violent quake. He struggled to hang on to his control as it shimmied through his grasp.

Unable to stand it any longer, he grasped Dixie by the shoulders and hauled her up against him, nearly crushing her in his embrace. She let out a grateful sigh as flesh pressed to flesh and he slanted his mouth across hers for a hot, hungry kiss. He wanted to consume her, to absorb her — each part of her, body and soul and secrets. The need to possess, to claim, to mate overwhelmed him. His hips rocked against Dixie's, but all he met with was the frustrating scrape of soft denim against his flesh.

Trailing kisses and nips down her throat, he reached down and wrestled with her jeans, dragging them down along with her silk and lace panties. He slid one hand between her thighs, threading his fingers through the soft nest of dark hair, seeking the moist warmth at the heart of her femininity. She lifted her hips, moving restlessly as he stroked and teased. His left hand swept down her back, over her jacket and the tails of her flannel shirt to the ripe curve of her bare buttock. He pulled her toward him as he slipped two fingers into her satiny heat.

Dixie cried out, her breath coming in pants and gasps. She clutched his shoulders, moving against him, needing, needing, needing. She whimpered and rubbed her head against his jaw.

"Oh, Jake, please, please, please," she panted. "I need you inside me. Please don't make me wait."

He growled in her ear, nuzzling through her thick hair to nip her earlobe. The velvety crown of his arousal nudged her belly and she brought a hand between them and tried to guide him. In the blink of an eye she was on her back on the blanket, with Jake looming over her, his blue eyes gleaming hot and dark.

"I want you, Dixie," he murmured, his voice a low husky rasp. "All of you."

She shivered as she looked up at him, knowing that he was asking her to lower the last of her barriers, that this would go beyond the joining of their bodies. He would become a part of her as she had allowed no one to become a part of her ever. She shivered again, not from the chill of the wind against her bare skin, but from the fear within her. She wanted him in her heart, in her soul, and it terrified her to need another person so badly. Old hurts had conditioned her against letting anyone that close and still she wanted Jake. That had to mean it was right, didn't it? That had to mean she was safe, that he was the one man who would take her heart and not break it, love her as she was and cherish her, didn't it?

She closed her eyes and prayed that it did. When she opened them and stared up into Jake's intense, waiting gaze, she said, "Yes."

Jake took in her answer, everything inside him going as still as the eye of a hurricane. He had promised himself he wouldn't push her, wouldn't drag from her what she wasn't ready to give. Still he had asked her to give him everything, not because he needed to master her, but because he loved her. Love was a humbling thing; it stripped away pride and control. He loved Dixie and wanted nothing more than for her to love him in return.

He looked into her eyes now, wide and clear, and saw everything he had hoped to see — love and need and hope. There was uncertainty there as well, and vulnerability, and they tugged at his heart.

"Love me, Jake," she whispered, her lips moist and trembling slightly. "I love you."

Relief flooded through him in a cool tide. He brushed his mouth against the curve of her cheek, smoothed her hair back with his fingertips. "Oh, baby," he murmured. "You don't know how I needed to hear you say that."

He kissed her lips, her chin. He pushed aside her jacket and shirt and kissed the tip of each breast, kissed the soft flesh below her navel and kissed her hips. With quick and gentle hands he divested them both of jeans and shoes. He stroked his hands down Dixie's legs, enjoying the silkiness of her skin. He ran his fingers over her feet, marveling at how small and dainty they were, how delicate the bones. He raised one and kissed the arch, trailing his tongue up to the sensitive hollow just behind the ankle.

Dixie lay back, watching him, absorbed his care and attention. He kissed a tiny mole on the inside of her knee as reverently as he kissed her lips, with as much passion as he gave her breasts. His hands stroked over her as if she were a priceless sculpture and he was memorizing every detail with his fingertips.

He parted her thighs and kissed her deeply, intimately, his tongue stroking and probing. Flames of desire leaped inside her, burning away patience and focusing her attention on the need that throbbed through her like a physical pain. Her back arched off the blanket and her fingers clutched at Jake's hair, tugging.

He reared up over her then, lifted her hips and filled her with a single thrust, pushing, pushing until she gasped. He brushed his lips against the shell of her ear, saying, "All of me, Dixie. I want you to take all of me, everything, and give me everything. I love you."

She breathed his name and tightened her fingers on the hard muscles of his back. "Yes. Yes."

They made love slowly, intensely, watching each other's eyes, concentrating on each sensation. The sky darkened to purple and the sun sank like a flaming ball, spreading fire across the horizon. The ocean roared and hissed.

Dixie felt completion rushing toward her as powerful and urgent as the surge of the sea, and in one corner of her heart, in the last bastion of her fear, she tried to hold it off for a moment, afraid of the power of it, afraid of what would come after. But it was beyond her strength to prevent it and the last wall of her defenses fell, battered down as wave after wave of sensation consumed her. Jake strained against her, his body rigid, a groan rumbling deep in his chest. He clutched her to him with a fierce embrace and Dixie answered him with one of her own, squeezing him tight, her heart pressing to his.

After a long moment he raised his head and looked down at her, brushing her hair back from her eyes, his expression tender but watchful. He was waiting for something. She could sense it. But she was too spent to try to figure out what it was. She let him look into her eyes, let him see everything she was feeling.

Finally he gave her a little smile and said, "I'm freezing my butt off. When did it get so cold out here?"

"It was always cold. We were just too pre-occupied to notice."

She flipped the edge of the blanket over him. He rolled onto his side with her in his arms, wrapping them together. "Yeah, I guess I had my mind on something else, like how much I love you."

"Why, Mr. Gannon, you have such a way with words," she drawled, batting her eyelashes in a perfect imitation of a debutante at a cotillion. "You ought to be a writer."

"You think so? I was thinking maybe I should do something with my hands," he said, winning a giggle from her as he tickled her. He sobered and kissed her, tenderly, deeply. When he lifted his head again he looked as serious as she'd ever seen him. "Dixie, I think we need to have a talk."

Panic coiled in her stomach. She had committed herself. She had promised him everything she was, everything she had been, but the prospect of telling him now made her shiver. She would tell him, she swore to herself, she would. She just needed a little more time to prepare, that was all. She had revealed much of her past already. She didn't think she had the strength for anything more today.

"Not on an empty stomach," she said, finding a smile for him. "I'm starved, aren't you?"

Jake sighed and sat up, letting the blanket pool at his waist. "Yeah," he murmured. "I'm starved too."

Starved for the truth. Dixie had promised him, but she was reneging now that the passion had come and gone. She was pulling back from him. It hurt.

"Don't be mad at me, Jake," she begged, sitting up beside him.

Her eyes were wide and smoky in the firelight, more golden than brown. They begged eloquently for understanding, for time. He caught himself cursing her for being such a damn good actress. She could twist his emotions into knots with nothing more than a look, a subtle nuance of expression.

She put a hand on his arm. "Please don't be mad. I know we need to talk. I just don't want it to be right now, okay? Everything has happened so fast. Let me catch my breath. We can talk ourselves hoarse tomorrow if you want. Just not tonight. Please?"

The tears were his undoing. He felt like a cad for pushing her even though he knew full well he hadn't pushed very hard or for anything unreasonable. He loved her. He deserved to have her tell him the truth. He wanted everything to be settled between them so they could forget about the past and look to the future. But those damn tears did him in. His resolve crumbled like a sand castle.

He gave Dixie a hug and kissed the top of her head. "So you're hungry, huh?"

"Famished."

"For food?"

She gave him a throaty chuckle. "For the moment."

Eleven

Dixie woke by slow degrees, her body sated, her mind numbed by the pleasant fog of dreams and memories of the night before. She burrowed deeper under the covers, her head nestling into a plump down pillow that smelled like Jake — warm, clean, masculine. She pulled the sheet and quilt up to her chin, sighing and smiling.

They had dined on the beach wrapped in their blanket and sitting as close to the fire as they dared. The picnic supper Jake had brought had consisted of cold breast of chicken, garlic bread, and a pasta salad he had made himself. They had shared a small bottle of white wine and fed each other bits of fudge, devoting much time to licking fingers and nibbling crumbs off each other's lips. Dixie had crowed over getting Jake to eat sugar and Jake had crowed over getting Dixie to eat a meal that hadn't been dunked in animal fat and fried to a crisp. They had declared the match a tie.

The ride back to Mare's Nest had seemed

to take forever. As the weather changed, the sea grew rougher. Dixie's little boat had bobbed like a piece of driftwood. She had been forced to devote her attention to getting them back in one piece when all she had wanted was a leisurely trip with plenty of time to look at the stars and enjoy the motion of the water. As it turned out there had been no stars and the motion of the water had been enough to make a seasoned sailor queasy.

There was bad weather coming in from somewhere. The wind had howled during the night and she could tell by the chill on the end of her nose that the temperature had fallen considerably. She turned, thinking to cuddle up to Jake, but he was gone. She vaguely remembered his kissing her forehead and slipping out of bed, saying something about his morning run. The man was a fanatic. She was definitely going to have to work some more on getting him to slow down and relax. This was one morning he could well have forgotten jogging and gotten his exercise in a much more enjoyable way.

Dixie stretched and smiled and burrowed down into the bed again. They had driven back from the marina to find Tyler Holt's pickup parked behind her house and the lights on in the attic windows. Without a word they had turned down the path and walked to Jake's cottage, dogs and cats trailing after them, only to be shut out on the porch.

She wondered if Delia and Tyler had cleared the air between them. She hoped so. She wanted her cousin to be happy. She also wanted her house back. Jake's bed wasn't nearly as comfortable as hers, a fact she could overlook while he was in it. When he was in bed with her she wasn't aware of anything but heat and pleasure and loving him so much she thought her heart would burst.

She sat up now and leaned back against the pillows, drawing her knees up and pulling the blankets to her chin. Gray light fell through the window like thick mist. Through the glass she could see the ocean was the color of granite, pitching with whitecaps, spitting foam against the shore. The sky hung down low, the leaden clouds rolling, their swollen bellies looking ready to burst. The sand of the beach was as white as bleached bones in comparison.

Abby hobbled nervously along a short stretch of beach with a stick in her mouth. She didn't like storms and was as good at predicting one as any meteorologist. Bob Dog watched her with a quizzical expression, bowing and prancing, trying unsuccessfully to entice her into a game. Three of Dixie's cats sat on the porch rail, lined up like milk bottles, their tails twitching.

There was no sign of Jake, but she knew he was out there, his long powerful legs eating up the shoreline, the wind in his hair, his intense blue eyes fixed on a distant point. How he had any energy left after last night was beyond her. All she wanted to do was stay in bed and cuddle with him for the rest of the day. She felt supremely lazy but forced herself to get up just the same.

She had put Jake off on the matter of their heart-to-heart, wanting more time to prepare herself. Now she thought about her plan for the morning, the nerves in her stomach doing a tap dance.

She would set the scene carefully. First she would shower and dress — her jeans and one of his shirts. Nothing remotely glamorous because she wanted the emphasis to be on who she was now, not who she had been. She would make a pot of coffee and bring over some of the cinnamon rolls she had baked the day before. And she would make wheat toast to appease his sense of nutrition. She would let him shower and dress and then they would sit down at the table and she would simply tell him.

It was no big deal. Being Devon Stafford

had been a job and she had left it. Jake had been in the Marine Corps and he had left it. Same thing. She would reveal all, get it over with, answer his questions, and then they could get on to the next phase of their relationship.

She showered in record time and dried her hair with Jake's blow dryer cranked on high. She ended up looking as if she had been trapped in a wind tunnel, her bob a wild bush around her head. She tried to press it down with her hands, then left it. Her hair was the least of her worries. After pulling on her jeans and a heavy brown plaid flannel shirt from Jake's closet, she ran to her house, tripping over cats and dogs on the way.

Tyler Holt's truck was still there. Either he and Delia had made up or she had killed him. Knowing them both, Dixie figured it was a fifty-fifty proposition.

"My God, Dixie, you look like somebody scared you," Sylvie said, swinging open the porch door. "What did you do to your hair?"

Dixie started and clutched a hand to her heart. "Cripes, Sylvie, you hadn't ought to jump out at people that way. You nearly gave me a heart attack." She trudged up the steps to the porch, stepping around a knot of kittens wrestling on the landing. She scowled at her friend. What are doing hiding up here anyway?"

Sylvie made an incredulous face and lifted her jewel-encrusted hands to the heavens. "What hiding? I wasn't hiding. I came to borrow some coffee. Can't a friend borrow a little coffee? Is this a crime in South Carolina now, to borrow coffee?"

Dixie gave her a steady look. "Coffee. Uh-huh. Your being here doesn't have a thing to do with finding out what happened between Tyler and Delia."

"Is Tyler here? I had no idea," she said, blinking innocently.

Dixie rolled her eyes and strode past her, weaving her way through the clutter toward the kitchen. The house was quiet except for Cyclops, who trotted after her howling for his breakfast.

"You don't fool me, Sylvie Lieberman," she said, scooping cat food out of a container on the counter and dumping it into an array of bowls on the floor. "You want to know if they made up or not."

"And you don't?"

" 'Course I hope they did. I hope Tyler had sense enough to tell Dee he still loves her even if she does look like a refugee from Chernobyl."

She opened a cupboard, yanked a can of

coffee and slammed the door shut before the junk crammed inside could fall on her in an avalanche.

"And what about you and Mr. Handsome?" Sylvie asked slyly. She peeked inside a plastic container on the table and snatched a cinnamon roll. "Did you tell him?"

"Not yet. I'm going to over breakfast."

"You'd better, dearie," Sylvie said, nibbling on her roll. "No good can come of keeping this secret from him."

Dixie leaned back against the counter and rubbed her temples. "Don't put any extra pressure on me here, Sylvie. I'm nervous already."

"It's just a little stage fright," Sylvie counseled, coming to wrap a slender arm around Dixie's shoulders. She gave her a motherly squeeze. "Everything will turn out fine. Trust me, I know these things. My Sid, God rest his soul, always said I had a sixth sense about people. Your Jake is a good one."

Dixie nibbled her lip, her brows furrowing. "I hope you're right, 'cause I'm so crazy in love with that man it scares me."

"So that's what's the matter with your hair."

"Your coffee," Dixie said, thrusting the can at her friend.

"Coffee?" Sylvie said blankly. "Oh, yeah. My coffee." She took it and tucked it in the crook of her arm like a football. She bussed Dixie's cheek and moved toward the door. "Thanks, love. Good luck."

"Sylvie?" Dixie gave her a tremulous smile. "Thanks for the pep talk. You're a good friend."

Sylvie sniffed. "Tell me something I don't already know."

Jake was trotting up to the cottage when Dixie returned with her cinnamon rolls. He slowed to a walk, wading through the mob of dogs fawning at his feet. He looked flushed and fit, like an ad for running gear. Dixie felt her stomach warm just looking at him as he bent to pat furry heads.

"Hey, lady," he said, grinning up at her, dimples flashing. "That looks like a shirt I used to own."

Dixie sniffed at him. "Well, you weren't there to put your arms around me when I woke up. This was the next best thing."

"I'm here now," he said, his voice low, rumbling with sensual promise.

He cupped the back of her head with one big hand and dropped a kiss to her mouth. He had intended it as a quick peck, but the instant their lips came together, it softened and deepened until both of them groaned at the pleasure of it. Bob Dog tried to wedge his nose between them, then sat down on the path beside them and let out a mournful howl.

"Jealous," Jake muttered. He tweaked Dixie's cheek and backed toward the steps. "I'll hit the shower, then we can have breakfast."

And talk, his gaze said plainly enough. Dixie sucked in a breath and nodded.

"I'll make some coffee."

"Great. Hey, did you change your hair?" He cast a quizzical glance over his shoulder. "It looks . . . bigger."

"Get in the shower, Gannon, before I sic my dogs on you."

The breakfast preparations took all of five minutes. Dixie wandered around the cottage listening to the sound of the shower running and the storm warnings coming over the radio. She was too nervous to sit, too nervous to eat. There was nothing in Jake's house to straighten even if she had been inclined to do so. The place was neat as a pin, looking like a writer's retreat to be featured in *Country Living* magazine. Even his desk was immaculate — typewriter covered, pens in their holder, blank paper neatly stacked.

She leaned over the top like a child who had been instructed to look but not touch.

She was curious about Jake's book, but she had promised to respect his superstition about not wanting other people to see it before it was ready. Still, if she could just accidentally catch a glimpse of a page or two . . . but there were no pages to be found. Writers on television were always portrayed with a wastebasket beside their desk overflowing with snowballs of wadded-up paper. Jake's wastebasket was cleaner than most of her house, not even a gum wrapper in evidence.

She turned her attention to the shelves above the desk. Jake had filled them with reference books and with the large cardboard box that contained his mysterious manuscript. The load was proving to be too much for the flimsy shelves. The screws were pulling loose at the top of the mounting strips. If they weren't tightened soon the whole works would come crashing down.

Digging a penknife out of her hip pocket Dixie climbed to her knees on the desktop. The instant she applied her makeshift screwdriver, the screw fell out. The mounting strip sprung away from the wall at the top. The shelves shifted ominously, then everything pitched downward like a rock slide. Dixie scrambled to the floor, clamping her hands to her head and wincing as books plummeted in a heap. The box tumbled like a boulder, careening off the desk. She lunged for it as it tipped, but it was too late. The thing had sprung open and papers spewed out.

"Oh, my Lord, he'll kill me!"

She dropped to her knees amid the rubble and frantically began scooping up papers to stuff back into the box. But her hands stilled as her brain slowly took in what she was looking at.

There were clippings from newspapers and magazines. Some old and yellow, some glossy white. Full pages and scraps of pages. All of them about one subject: Devon Stafford.

Dixie felt a cold lump of dread settle in her stomach. Her hands sifted through the mess on their own, as if they belonged to someone else. Stunned, she watched them as they turned over picture after picture of herself, of the image she had left behind. Colored photos, black and white photos, publicity shots and candid shots snapped by the paparazzi.

Someone had jotted notes on several of the photos in black marker. *What if she dyed her hair? Cut it?* In one a big, thick circle had been drawn around the golden sea star she wore even now at her throat. She lifted her hand to touch the charm, as if to comfort it even though it had betrayed her.

There were reams of handwritten and typed notes, all spread around her now like abandoned Christmas wrapping. Questions and conjecture on the disappearance of a sex symbol.

Jake was writing a mystery all right, and the mystery was her.

Dixie's vision clouded with tears. He'd known all along. Somehow he had tracked her to Mare's Nest and he had been watching her, gathering his facts, researching his topic — in depth. Her stomach gave a sick lurch and she pressed one arm over it as if she'd taken a blow.

He'd known. Jake Gannon hadn't fallen in love with Dixie La Fontaine. He had come here obsessed with Devon Stafford and he'd found her. She had taken him into her home, into her heart, God help her, into her body, and he was nothing but another man looking to capture a star.

He had turned the tables on her as neatly as could be. She had gone on thinking she was so smart, such a consummate actress that no one would ever guess. Well, she was an amateur compared to Jake Gannon. He had played the part of a man in love and she had bought the act hook, line, and sinker.

From the corner of her eye she saw him

stop in the doorway between the bedroom and living room. He was barefoot in jeans and a navy blue fisherman's sweater, his hair damp and finger-combed. He closed his eyes as if against a stabbing pain and swore softly under his breath. Dixie stayed where she was, the centerpiece among the display of damning evidence.

Jake took a hesitant step forward. "Dixie, I can explain —"

"I'll bet you can." She sifted papers through her hands and let them scatter across the hardwood floor. "Just like you explained why you came here. Just like you explained how you love me."

"Dixie —"

"Oh, you're real good with words, Jake," she said, staring at a picture of her former self — gorgeous, sexy, blond, slim, an apparition, an aberration, a woman she had grown to hate. "I believed every line you fed me."

"It's not what you think."

"Isn't it?" She pushed herself to her feet and dusted her hands on the tails of the shirt she'd borrowed from him. "Well, I'll tell you what I think. I think you came here looking for Devon Stafford, and I think you came here planning to write about her and make a wheelbarrow full of money. Are you gonna tell me that's not true? Because if you are I think it might be the first time I won't believe you."

She glared at him, tears brimming in her eyes. She refused to let them fall, calling on her reserve of pride. Her voice went hoarse with the effort to hold her devastation in check. "You gonna tell me that, Jake? Huh? You gonna tell me you didn't come here looking for Devon Stafford?"

His silence was as damning as any confession. He hung his head, having the grace or the shrewd sense to look contrite. Dixie cursed herself. She wanted him to deny it. She wanted him to explain it away. But she knew there was only one explanation.

She pushed at a pile of photographs with the toe of her sneaker. "Tell me, what's the going rate on stories about me now? I used to be worth big bucks. A tabloid offered half a million for a scoop when I first left Hollywood. That would fill your garage right up with Porsches, wouldn't it?"

"It's not like that," he said tightly, the muscles in his jaw working furiously.

"It's not like that," Dixie repeated softly.

She took a couple of steps toward him, her arms crossed defensively over her chest. "You want to know what it's like, Jake? You want to know what it's like to have people hound you night and day because they think you're something different, because they think you're some kind of goddess when everything you are is just a lie? You want to know what it's like to have people want to touch you, not because you're anyone special inside, but because you're a star? You want to know what it's like to have your best friend kill herself because she can't be you? You want to know what it's like to have a man tell you he loves you and then find out it's not you he's making love to, it's some dead glossy image he wants to make a buck off?"

The tears streamed down her face unchecked now. She had edged closer and closer to him as she'd spoken, until she was standing right under his nose. She stared up at him, trembling with fury and hurt, her hands clenching into fists at her sides.

"Did you get a big kick out of it, Jake? Did you close your eyes and think of Devon Stafford while you were doing it?"

"No."

"You bastard!" she shrieked, pounding his chest with her fists. "You lying bastard!"

"Dixie, I love you."

She slapped him as hard as she could.

"How dare you say that to me," she said, stepping back from him. "How dare you.

What do you take me for? Am I such a pa-thetic little thing you think you can buy me back with a few pretty words?"

He winced more at the sting of her words than at the blow she'd delivered. He stepped toward her, his laser-blue gaze never leaving her eyes. "I love you, Dixie. It's the truth. If you'll just let me explain —"

"I've seen the explanation, Jake," she said, gesturing to the mess on the floor. "When were you going to tell me — the day the book hit the stands? Maybe you were gonna invite me to an autographing. That would have been a nice freak show. Parade me in front of the public and let them marvel at what their perfect woman turned into after all the glitter faded."

"Stop it," Jake ordered. He grabbed her by the arms, his fingers biting into her flesh through the heavy flannel shirt. "Just stop it. Let me get two words in, will you?"

She glared up at him. "You want two words? I've got two words for you, but since you've already done it to me, I'll spare my-self the trouble of saying them."

She kicked him hard in the shin and bolted for the door the instant he let go of her.

Jake hobbled after her, swearing under his breath, limping heavily. He stumbled out onto the porch and down the steps. Dixie ran ahead of him, her hair bobbing, the long tails of his shirt streaming behind her. He closed ground on her easily, even though he was barefoot and hurting. Then Bob Dog bounded onto the path directly in front of him, cutting his legs out from under him and sending him flying.

He hit the path with a thud, landing on his belly, and came up spitting sand. He shook his head to clear it, then looked for Dixie. She was already rounding her house, making a beeline for her truck.

He sat up, swearing a blue streak. The German shepherd stood a few feet away, bowing and barking at him. Jake scooped up a handful of sand and flung it at the dog, who cut off his barking, gave Jake a hurt look and slinked away with his tail down. Hobbit came to sit on the path directly in front of him, the little corgi perking his triangular ears. Honey and Abby stood to the side, staring at him. They seemed to know he'd hurt their mistress and they glared at him with accusing brown eyes.

Jake cradled his head in his hands, feeling more lost and miserable than he'd ever felt in his life. He'd blown it royally. He hadn't seen any way to tell Dixie about his original purpose in coming here, especially when she hadn't been willing to tell him about her past. He had wanted her trust, had felt hurt that she hadn't given it to him. Now she might never give it to him.

"I did know you from somewhere," Sylvie said quietly. She stood beside the path, her slender form swallowed up by the yellow slicker she wore against the increasing wind. It was apparent from the look on her face that she had listened in on part of the row. "A. J. Campion, the biography writer. I knew it would come to me. Too bad it didn't come sooner."

Jake pushed himself to his feet. "Sylvie, I know this looks bad, but I swear to you I love her. I love Dixie. I don't care who she used to be. I love who she is."

"You broke her heart."

"I didn't mean to."

"What did you mean to do, Jake?" she asked with a shrug. "Write a story? Is that what you came here for? Did it ever occur to you that she wanted to be left alone?"

"I wanted to know why. I wanted her to tell me in her own way, in her own words. If you know who I am, then you know how I write. It would have been her own story, not some sleazy exposé." He slicked back his damp hair, gritty now with sand. "But I don't give a damn about the book now. I don't care if the rest of the world never finds out about Devon Stafford. I want Dixie. I love Dixie. Help me get her back, Sylvie."

Sylvie looked at him a long moment, weighing his words and the sincerity behind them. She stared long and hard, her arms wrapped around herself, shoulders hunched against the wind that buffeted her and tore at her hair.

"This I can't do, Jake," she said, shaking her head. "This is between you and Dixie. I told her to tell you about herself. I told her no good would come of keeping secrets. So you're the one I should have been telling this to. Now you've broken her heart. I don't know if anyone can fix that, Jake. You don't know how fragile she was when she came here, how badly she needed people to love her. This hurt you've given her . . . I don't know what I can do."

"You can loan me your car keys."

Twelve

Dixie drove without regard for traffic laws or the worn-out shocks in her Bronco. She sent the truck hurling up the old coast road, and it bucked and pitched over bumps and potholes. On the seat beside her Cyclops bounced like a scruffy furball, digging his claws into the upholstery. The cat complained loudly, his squawks and howls like an out-of-tune oboe concerto. Dixie paid him no mind. She clutched the steering wheel, occasionally jerking one hand away to swipe at the tears pouring from her eyes. Her ragged sobs and jerky breaths accompanied the cat's discordant wails, making a racket that hurt her ears.

Yet another warning about the approaching storm came over the radio. Dixie switched it off. She didn't care if it stormed. She hoped it stormed to beat Hades. It would be nothing to rival the storm raging inside her now. Mother Nature would be put to shame by comparison.

Blast it all, why had she trusted Jake Gannon? Why had she allowed herself to fall in love with him? She'd known the minute she'd laid eyes on him and his Porsche that he would be nothing but trouble. She'd spotted him right off for a perfectionist. Men like that didn't go for women like her, they went for women like Devon Stafford.

What had he thought — that he could entice her into returning to her former self? That he could bribe her with his love, bribe her into starving herself and suffering collagen injections? Had he believed she would go through all that to make him happy, the way Tyler Holt had with Delia? Had he wanted that badly to be seen with a sex symbol? Or had his sole purpose been getting his story?

What difference did it make? Either way he'd played her for a fool and she'd fallen for it headfirst. Lord, she really was a pathetic little thing, needing his love so badly she would believe anything he told her.

Choking on her tears, Dixie slanted the truck into a parking spot and hit the brakes. The tires had barely stopped squealing before she slid from the driver's seat. Cyclops flung himself on her chest, and she hurried along the wooden walk of the marina, wearing her ugly cat like a necklace.

Fabiano burst out of the bait shop as she neared the door. A black leather vest was his only concession to the biting cold of the wind; his magnificent chest and arms were bare, as usual. He stepped into her path, the wind tearing at his long hair, his zealot's eyes fastened on her face.

"Where are you going, my Dixie?" he asked. "What is it that makes you be crying?"

Dixie glared up at him, sniffling, but he refused to let her pass. "I'm crying because I hurt," she said defensively. "Do you want to make something of it?"

"Dixie, Dixie," he cooed, reaching for her, concern etching his brow. Cyclops hissed at him and batted at his hand. Fabiano withdrew, giving the cat a wary look. "What is making this hurt inside you? Jake Gannon?"

She refused to answer, which was an answer in itself. She looked off toward the boats that bobbed like corks in the harbor, wiping her nose with her hand and smacking Cyclops in the head in the process. The cat yodeled a protest, jumped down from her and scampered sideways down the dock like a crab.

Fabiano put his big hands on Dixie's shoulders and gave her a grave look. "I will kill him, ya?"

"Yeah, you go on ahead and kill him, Fabiano," she said sarcastically. "That's not gonna solve my problems."

She pulled away from him and tried to step around him. He blocked her path like a moving pillar of stone. "This is no day for the boat," he said sternly. "The storm is coming."

"Good. Fine. But I'm going out in my boat and I don't care if the thing sinks."

"Dixie! Dixie, wait!"

Dixie squeezed her eyes shut and stamped her foot as her heart gave a terrible lurch at the shouts that came from the parking lot. Jake came running toward them, his sneakers pounding on the boards of the walkway. Dixie turned toward him, setting her face in its sternest, most furious expression.

"Leave me alone."

"Honey, please," Jake said, stopping in front of her. "Let's go someplace and talk."

Dixie did her best to shut out thoughts of how he looked a little frazzled and very intense. She focused on her hurt and anger and drew on those emotions to sustain her. "I'm not talking to you. Anything I say could end up on the front page of a tabloid. There I'd be — a picture of my head slapped on someone else's body, right next to a story about Dojo the wild dog boy of the Ozarks."

Jake squeezed the bridge of his nose and heaved a much-put-upon sigh. "Dammit, Dixie, I don't write for the tabloids! I didn't come here to exploit you. Would you just give me a chance to explain?"

Fabiano stepped around Dixie, completely obscuring her from Jake's view. "It is best for you to leave now, Jake. Our Dixie doesn't need nothing from a man who would break her heart."

Jake ground his teeth, wrestling with his impatience. "Look, Fabiano, will you just butt out? This is none of your business."

Fabiano gave him a shrug and a roguish smile. "Our Dixie is my business. She is my friend, ya? I look out for her."

"Yeah, you and everybody else," Jake grumbled. He tried to step around the big man, but Fabiano moved with him. They eyed each other like wrestlers squaring off.

"I appreciate that everybody loves Dixie," Jake said. "But I love her too and I need a chance to talk to her, so back off. I don't want to have to hurt you here, pal, but my temper is running on a real lean mix right now."

"Hurt me?" Fabiano gave a derisive, arrogant laugh. He took one menacing step toward Jake and Jake laid him flat with one punch. The big man hit the dock like a felled sequoia. Dixie gasped and dropped down beside him on her knees.

"Fabiano! Are you all right?" She bit her

lip nervously and fussed at him, touching his hair, his shoulder. "Are you hurt?"

He groaned and came up on all fours, shaking his shaggy head slowly from side to side like a bull. Dixie glared at Jake and scrambled to her feet.

"You big bully!" She rushed up to him to smack him on the chest with her fist. "Who do you think you are, beating up on my friends?"

"He had fair warning."

"Oh! Fair! Like you would know the meaning of the word! Why don't you just get in your Porsche and go back to California where everything is pretty and perfect, just the way you like it."

"I'm not going back. I'm not going anywhere until I convince you that I love you."

"Then you'll be here until your teeth fall out."

She turned and stomped down the dock, abandoning her fallen giant and calling for her cat. Jake rushed after her. The rain was starting to fall. Cold, hard pellets hurled down out of an angry-looking sky. The wind howled and whistled through the bare masts of sailboats that tugged at their moorings. Thunder rumbled overhead. Dixie fumbled with the lock on the gate at her pier, but managed to get it open and slammed shut before Jake could push through it. He merely scaled the thing, dropping down on the other side and stalking after her again.

"Dammit, Dixie," he yelled above the wind. "You can't go out in this!"

"Don't tell me what I can and can't do, Jake Gannon!" she shouted back, stopping at her slip.

Jake grabbed her and swung her around to face him. "Will you use a little common sense? If you go out in this weather you're going to get yourself killed. Is that what you want? You want to kill yourself because you think I'm a bastard?"

She stared up at him, working hard to maintain the defiance in her eyes and not let him see the scrap of the fear his question had aroused in her. A gust of wind drove the rain down harder, slanting it at an angle that made it cut like a knife against bare skin. It whipped her hair, and the wet strands slapped her face. Her shirt was soaked, sticking to her body. Lightning cracked across the sky. Beyond the shelter of the harbor the sea was churning and heaving, growing rougher by the minute.

Had she really thought to go out in that?

Her first instinct had been to escape, to run away from the hurt, from the shame of her own weakness, from Jake and the threat he now posed to her peaceful life. But had he really driven her to self-destruction?

No, she thought, gathering her strength. She would stand her ground and endure whatever was to come. Mare's Nest was her home. She wouldn't let herself be driven from it. She was happy here. Yes, there would be a stampede of press once the story broke, but the furor would eventually die down and they would move on to stories more sensational than a star who had left Hollywood to get fat and live in an old house with a bunch of stray animals. She had run from her problems in California. She had run from her unhappiness. But now she had found herself and she wasn't running anymore.

She pulled herself back from the insanity of what she had been about to do. She pulled herself back from Jake. She dug the boat keys out of her pocket and tossed them to him, a wry smirk tipping up the corner of her mouth.

"No," she said. "On second thought, I'd rather you go out. Say hello to King Neptune for me."

With her head held high and her shoulders square, she turned and walked away, Cyclops dashing after her with his crooked tail raised like a flag.

★ ★ ★

"You love her, my friend?" Fabiano asked, pouring clear liquid from a slim bottle into two shot glasses on the table.

Jake stared at the glasses and the marred surface of the tabletop. They sat in the bait shop where it was warm and dry though rather aromatic. The clerk was filling in for the cook up the street at Clem's seafood place. Fabiano was filling in for the clerk. All around them, examples of Clem's prowess as a taxidermist stared with wild and beady glass eyes.

"I love her," Jake said. He tossed back half of his drink, shuddered and twitched and tried to focus his eyes. The stuff went down like acid and left a hot sweet aftertaste of licorice. When he spoke again his voice was as rough as gravel. "I love her more than life. I love her more than my Porsche. I love her more than anything." He finished off the drink and gasped for air. "Jeez, what is this stuff — paint thinner?"

"Homemade ouzo," Fabiano said with a proud grin. He slapped his massive bare chest with the palm of his hand. "Is good, ya? A real man's drink."

"Yeah. Remember to have that engraved on my tombstone."

Fabiano threw his head back and let go of

a laugh that shook the rafters. Jake turned his head and frowned at a stuffed weasel that was posed on its hind legs in a contortion of rage, baring needle-like teeth at him. He stared glumly past the creature and out the window. The rain poured down relentlessly in cold sheets. The wind shook the palmetto trees as easily as if they were pompoms. Thunder rumbled and lightning cracked in a violent duet. There wasn't a soul on the street, only a few abandoned cars along the curbs where the runoff swirled in a frothing torrent. At the moment the world looked about as desolate as he felt.

"How's the jaw?" he asked.

Fabiano made a face and gave a dismissing motion with his hand. He evidently viewed getting belted as a normal male bonding ritual. Jake had spotted him standing on the dock as he'd started to follow Dixie away from the boat and had prepared himself mentally for a battle that hadn't materialized. The artist had merely grinned at him, clamped a big hand on his shoulder and steered him into the pungent interior of the bait shop where they had discussed the situation like old friends.

"I need a plan here, pal," Jake said with a sigh.

Fabiano nodded. "Dixie is over at the Magnolia Bar. This is where everyone goes when a bad storm comes. It's tradition. They talk, tell stories, watch the Fortune Wheel on the big screen — the Trulove sisters bring videotapes."

Jake glanced across the street at the parking lot of the Magnolia Bar where pickups huddled side by side in the rain. Dixie's Bronco was there, as was Tyler Holt's black pickup.

"She's got a gun," Jake mused, rubbing his chin. "Do you think she'd shoot me in front of witnesses?"

Fabiano shook his head. "I don't think she'll shoot you. Not bad anyway. She loves you."

Jake gave a harsh laugh. "She hates my guts right now."

"Love. Hate." Fabiano's gigantic shoulders rose and fell. He narrowed his eyes and leaned toward Jake in a posture of conspiracy. "These are many times much the same thing. She loves you so she gives to you her heart. Now she thinks you are playing the games with her. She's angry — with you, with herself, because she trusted you. You must show her her trust was not misplaced."

This seemed awfully sage advice from a

man who was noticeably without female companionship, but Jake refrained from commenting.

"Yeah, well, that's easier said than done," he grumbled. He propped his chin in his hand and absently reached out and stroked the snarling weasel as he thought.

Regardless of the source, it was sound advice. Dixie's fragile trust in him lay in scattered shreds like the damning papers and pictures that had fallen from their box to the floor of his cottage. She was too hurt to listen to him, too furious to even look at him without being driven to violence. He had to show her.

Show her.

He came to attention suddenly in his chair, excitement crackling inside him like static electricity. He snatched up the weasel by its throat and thrust it over his head like a trophy, shouting, "Yes! Yes! I've got it!"

He turned toward Fabiano, pointing at him with the snarling animal. "What kind of artist are you?"

Fabiano leaned back away from the weasel, regarding Jake with a wary look. He pursed his lips and shrugged. "I paint, I sketch, I do a little sculpture."

"How long do you think they'll all stay at the Magnolia Bar?"

"Well into the night. This is a big storm."

Jake rose from his chair decisively. He tapped the weasel's head against the big man's shoulder and smiled like a champion, dimples flashing. "How would you like to do me a great big favor, *amigo?*"

"You're sure you don't want company tonight, Dixie?" Sylvie asked for the third time. "Now that Delia has made up with that schmuck Tyler and gone back to Myrtle Beach, you'll be all alone. Are you sure you don't want me to stay the night? I'd be more than happy to stay. Even though my sinuses would kill me from all those cats you keep and my lumbago acts up when I don't sleep in my own bed, I would stay with you. This is what friends are for."

Dixie pulled the key from the truck's ignition and stared up at her big empty house. She'd been with friends all day and half the night and she'd never felt more alone or more miserable since Jeanne had died.

They had been nothing but supportive, as they had always been with her. Leo and Macy Vencour had consoled her with quiet talk. The Trulove sisters had consoled her with chocolate pecan pie and ten rousing episodes of *Wheel of Fortune*. Eldon had offered to set Jake's Porsche ablaze and let the volunteer rescue squad have at it with fire hoses. None of them had managed to make her feel any better.

When it came right down to it, there was nothing anyone could do to heal the hurt of discovering someone you loved had been using you. That was something that required a long and painful recovery process. She knew; she'd been through it before, more than once.

The pain welled up again inside her and pressed at the backs of her eyes. Why, oh why, couldn't a man just love her for herself?

With an effort she sniffed back the tears. "No thanks, Sylvie. I really kind of need to be alone tonight."

Sylvie frowned and patted Dixie's shoulder. "I understand." She gathered her handbag and tugged down the brim of her rain hat. "Remember, it's always darkest before the dawn. My Sid, God rest his soul, used to say that all the time. He drove me crazy saying that, but a lot of times he was right. I think maybe this is one of those times."

Dixie couldn't find her voice to make a comment. She couldn't see how this cloud could have a silver lining, how the darkness in her heart would ever see the dawn, but she was too tired to argue.

Sylvie climbed out of the Bronco, complaining enthusiastically about the height of the thing, then hurried off down the dark path toward her cottage.

The storm had lost its fury, though the rain continued and occasional flashes of lightning brightened the sky. Dixie didn't bother with rain gear. She slid down out of the truck and walked across the yard, letting the rain wet her hair and dampen her new red Magnolia Bar sweatshirt. Her sneakers squished. In her arms she carried the shirt she had borrowed from Jake's closet that morning, wadded up and still wet from the soaking she'd gotten. She climbed the stairs to her house alone, her pets choosing to stay dry under the house rather than greet their mistress with their usual enthusiasm. Only Cyclops darted up the stairs after her, squeezing through the door before she had opened it more than a crack.

Dixie reached for the light switch beside the living room door, but her hand stilled before she turned it on. There were three candles burning on the coffee table, tall ivory tapers in brass candlesticks. All the magazines and baseball card albums had been cleared away. The mahogany table had been polished and shone like a moonlit lake. Beside the candles sat a box all done up in red and gold foil wrapping paper.

She dropped the shirt and went to sit on the couch. She stared at the box for a moment, nibbling on her lip and combing back her wet bangs with her fingers. It was obviously from Jake. No one else would have bothered to dust the table. The box was perfectly wrapped, the candles perfectly placed. A going-away present. A little something for her trouble.

She told herself she shouldn't open it, but she had never in her life been able to resist a present and she watched her hands creep toward it even as she told them to leave the thing alone.

Slowly she undid the wrappings, then lifted the lid and set it aside. She inched forward on the sofa cushion to peer into the box as cautiously as if she expected a snake to leap out of it. But she didn't draw back when she saw what was inside. She caught her breath in a surprised gasp and reached in carefully for the gift.

It was a book. A handmade book. The cover was a pen-and-ink drawing of a fairytale princess on a magnificent gray horse with small animals running alongside. It was done in a style that reminded her of medieval paintings, beautiful and intricate, filled with whimsical details. There were touches of watercolor throughout, sheer, soft colors that had rippled the page slightly, giving the animals a three-dimensional look. There was no title, and the story began immediately on the next page.

"Once upon a time there was a beautiful princess named Devon. All the people in the kingdom loved her because she was so beautiful, but Princess Devon was sad. She thought no one loved her for what was in her heart, so one day she ran away from her kingdom. . . ."

Her voice trailed away as she turned the page. She sat on the edge of the old couch with the thin manuscript resting on her knees, and read by the light of the beeswax candles. The story told of the knight who had set out on a quest to find the princess. Through magic the princess had taken the form of another woman and was living in a small kingdom by the sea. She had become a friend to all the people there and to all the small animals. Everyone had grown to love her for her kind heart and sweet nature.

The knight fell deeply in love with her, never suspecting she was the woman he had come in search for. When a butterfly told him she was in fact the princess, he didn't know what to do. He couldn't tell her he had come looking for the princess when she was the only one in his heart. His quest no longer mattered to him, because he had found something far more special than a princess people loved only for her beauty. He had found true love.

He decided to give her time, to gain her trust, to let her tell him her secret herself. But before that could happen she found him out. Thinking he had only been interested in capturing the beautiful princess to claim the reward, she sent him away.

That was where the story ended, with a drawing of the knight leading his horse away, both of them hanging their heads.

Dixie stared at the drawing through a mist of tears, her heart tearing in two. Jake. Her perfect golden knight. She hadn't given him a chance to explain. The evidence had been so damning, so hurtful. Even now she trembled as she struggled with the need to believe in him and the fear of being hurt again. She clutched the manuscript in her hands and bit her lip as tears of pain and confusion gathered in her eyes and rolled down her cheeks.

"I haven't settled on an ending yet," Jake said. He materialized out of the blackness of the dining room, cradling a purring Cyclops in his arms. He stroked the cat with a steady hand, but his gaze, that burning blue gaze, was on Dixie. She felt it reach past her barriers, clear to her soul. "I'm leaving it up to you. Either the princess sees the true depth of his love or she sends him away to die of a broken heart."

Dixie just looked at him and said nothing. She watched him set the cat down and kneel before the fireplace to set a match to the kindling on the grate. As the flames licked upward he reached into a cardboard box beside the hearth and pulled out several photographs. He fed them to the fire, watching as they curled in on themselves and disintegrated.

"I'm voting for the first ending, myself," he said quietly, reaching into the box for a handful of newspaper clippings. "But it's your book and you can do whatever you like with it."

He fed articles to the greedy orange flames. The light from the fire turned his handsome face bronze and made his hair shine like gold. Dixie's heart pounded. Robert Redford had nothing on this man, not even in his heyday. And he was either totally sincere or he was the best actor she'd ever played with.

Dixie's fingers curled tightly around the edge of the manuscript as she faced what was in her heart. The truth of the matter was she was bound to love him whether he was guilty or not, whether he was perfect or not. Her only choice seemed to be whether she would brave a chance at letting him hurt her more or suffer alone.

"It's a good book." She stroked the pages. "Based on a true story, isn't it? I like a book that's based on a true story."

Jake abandoned the fire and turned to look at her once again. "Do you like a happy ending?"

"When I can get one," she said cautiously.

"You can get one now."

He left the hearth and came around the table to kneel at her feet and gaze up into her eyes. "I love you, Dixie. I don't know how else to tell you."

"You came looking for Devon Stafford."

"She doesn't hold a candle to the lady who ran away with my heart."

"What about the story you came here to write?"

"I don't give a damn about that book. I wanted to find out who Devon Stafford really was, what it was that made her shine from the inside out. Now I know, but I don't want to share it with the rest of the world." He reached up and touched her cheek, giving her a tender smile. "See? I'm not perfect, I'm greedy. I want you all to myself."

Dixie's lips turned up at the corners. She

tapped a finger on the manuscript. "You made a couple of typos in here too."

Jake grinned, flashing his dimples and his straight white teeth. "Only a couple? I typed like a madman by candlelight all afternoon. I think I gave myself arthritis. I can't tell you how many times I got my fingers caught in the keys."

"Yeah, well, you aren't much with machines," she said, chuckling as he shot her a mock scowl. She stroked a hand over the cover of the book again, marveling at its beauty. She touched the signature beneath one of the horse's hooves. "Fabiano did the cover and the illustrations?"

"Yeah. He went into an artistic fit because he claimed the cover wasn't perfect. He wasn't going to let me have it, but I told him you were the last person who would care if the cat's ears weren't quite right."

"Guess you know me pretty well," she said softly.

"Not as well as I will if you marry me and let me hang around for the next fifty or sixty years. That's what I really want. That's all I want from you — your heart, your love. You, Dixie, not some platinum idol. Trust me to love you for who you are, honey. Please."

She shivered at the sincerity in his eyes, her soul craving to believe him. "You don't care that I don't look like Devon Stafford anymore?"

"Not a bit."

"You don't care that I take in every stray that comes down the pike?"

He shook his head. "Not much."

"You don't care that I'm a hopeless slob of a housekeeper?"

His smile tightened. "We'll talk about that."

Dixie laughed. She looked at Jake long and hard, taking in everything about him — the lines of his face, the rigid set of his broad shoulders, the steady, searching quality of his gaze. She would never be able to hide much from him. He looked past every act, every mask, to the woman she was inside.

Wasn't that what she had wanted all along? A man to love her for what was inside her.

Here he was kneeling at her feet with a one-eyed cat crawling up his thigh. How could she not love him? How could she not take that chance? She had already given him her heart. What would her life be without it?

Trust me to love you for who you are. . . .

She reached out a hand and brushed the golden hair that fell across his forehead. "You're too good to be true," she whispered.

"No," he said. "But I'm the man who loves you, Dixie. Please don't push me away."

She closed her eyes and took a deep breath. She loved him. She needed him. She had vowed to give him everything she was, everything she had been, everything that was in her heart. It was time to take that step.

With a trembling smile she lowered her mouth to his and whispered, "What do you say we go to work on that happy ending?"

The employees of Thorndike Press hope you have enjoyed this Large Print book. All our Large Print titles are designed for easy reading, and all our books are made to last. Other Thorndike Press Large Print books are available at your library, through selected bookstores, or directly from us.

For information about titles, please call:

(800) 223-1244
(800) 223-6121

To share your comments, please write:

Publisher
Thorndike Press
295 Kennedy Memorial Drive
Waterville, ME 04901